MONTANA BIGFOOT CAMPFIRE STORIES

RUSTY WILSON

Yellow Cat
PUBLISHING

For all who love adventure, mystery, and the beautiful wilderness of Montana

CONTENTS

FOREWORD

Ever thought about visiting the beautiful and rugged state of Montana? If so, be sure to read these stories before you go, for there may be more there than you ever imagined in your wildest dreams.

These all new stories are sure to make you want to hide deep in your sleeping bag if you're brave enough to read them at night by headlamp while camped in one of the state's beautiful campgrounds. And what just brushed against your tent? A wolf? Grizzly bear? Or was it something even bigger and more terrifying?

Fly-fishing guide Rusty Wilson, known as the World's Greatest Bigfoot Story Teller, has spent years collecting these tales from his clients around the campfire, stories guaranteed to make sure you won't want to go out after dark.

Come join a botanist in Glacier National Park who discovers a most unusual use for a mudpack, then watch a strange sight in the Sweet Grass Hills of northern Montana. Come along as a tow-truck driver tries to figure out why a tourist won't abandon his car in the winter cold, then join a campground host as he faces his deepest fears.

And if you survive all that, come along on an experiment in terror in a resort in the wilds. Next, join in the discovery of a very unusual find on a dinosaur dig in Montana's badlands, then learn why it's not a good idea to feed the wildlife, nor to harass them. Climb a tall peak with a filmmaker to discover a terrifying and dangerous sight that almost costs him his life, and finally, visit with a musician as he discovers the real meaning of an appreciative audience.

You'll want to be sure you're not alone in the woods while reading these stories, or maybe even alone inside your house!

Another great book from Rusty Wilson, Bigfoot expert and story-teller—tales for both the Bigfoot believer and those who just enjoy a good story.

INTRODUCTION

Greetings, fellow adventurers, to another collection of Bigfoot camp-fire stories featuring one of our country's wildest states, Montana. And because it borders Canada, there are also lots of deep forests and wildlands for our big friends to inhabit nearby, as they don't need passports.

If you've never been to Montana, it should be on your list, for there's no place like it. From its eastern high-grass prairies to the lofty Rockies of Glacier National Park, there's plenty of variety to suit all tastes, human or otherwise.

And don't forget that a small portion of the state is in Yellowstone National Park, the location of a number of great Bigfoot sightings, some recounted in my book, *Yellowstone Bigfoot Campfire Stories*. The Greater Yellowstone Ecosystem covers a good portion of the southern part of Montana, including the Bitterroot and Tobacco Root Mountains, and you'll find that a number of the stories in this book take place in that region. Perhaps the Bigfoot in these stories are the relatives of those in Yellowstone, or maybe even the same ones, for who knows how extensive the Bigfoot range is?

Even though my home base is Colorado, I have a good friend who has a fly-fishing business in southern Montana, and because I love fishing the fine waters of that state, I often go up there for part of the summer to help him out, as well as to just enjoy the beauty of a place still wild and free. I love Colorado, but there's no place like Montana, and I cherish my many experiences and good times there.

Like most of my stories, these were collected around campfires from my fly-fishing clients, though some were told to me in person. There's nothing like being outdoors around a fire to get folks talking, especially if you add in some mouth-watering Dutch-oven cooking. Some were told in Colorado, even though they took place in Montana, while some were told while I was guiding up there. And though some of my other books have Montana stories, these are all new.

If I were a Bigfoot, I would head for Montana, simply because it has tons of places still untouched by humans. I believe that the Bigfoot species is on the brink of extinction in many parts of our country as more and more places are developed, but Montana still offers plenty of space and good habitat—and the fishing is unparalleled—and yes, I think Bigfoot do fish, though not with a rod and reel. The winters can be a bit brutal when the Polar Vortex sweeps down, but in general, it's a good place for them.

So, sit back with a cup of hot chocolate in a big comfy chair or by a campfire and enjoy. Get out a map and follow along, then make plans to visit, but when you do, keep your eyes and ears open for North America's most unique and elusive creature, for your odds of seeing them are pretty darn good in what's known as the Treasure State. —Rusty

1

THE MUDPACK

I met Kelly while fishing on the beautiful Yampa River down near Split Mountain in northwest Colorado near Dinosaur National Monument.

Sarah and I had taken the weekend off and gone to see the famous dinosaur quarry, then I had to give the fishing a shot there on the Yampa at an old family fishing hole that my grandfather once frequented. He wasn't a fly-fisherman, like I am, but would just bait a hook with a worm and toss it into the water, kind of old school, and he always had great success.

I didn't catch one fish, but I did meet Kelly, who was hanging around waiting for his girlfriend to show up. She was on her way back from seeing a herd of wild horses with a friend who lived in nearby Vernal, Utah. As a botanist, Kelly had decided he'd prefer to hang out by the river and take photos of the wildflowers.

I was glad he had, after hearing this story, for I don't think I would've met him otherwise. —Rusty

Rusty, I used to work for Glacier National Park as a seasonal botanist, and I hope you'll mention that Glacier was where this actually happened. Since Glacier is getting to be so popular, people need to know what's out there. There's much more than the infamous grizzly bears you're told to watch out for.

My job that fateful summer was to help do a survey of invasive plants in the park. We always worked together in teams of two, mostly for safety reasons, as bears are less likely to harass groups of people. Even though a pair isn't really a group, the park was trying to accomplish its objectives on a budget, yet they didn't want us out there working alone.

And if my partner in crime hadn't been sick from a case of giardia, I wouldn't have been alone that particular day, and this probably wouldn't have happened, but who's to say? My co-worker's water filter quit working, and he got sick.

This was the second week he'd been out sick, so by then I was used to being alone. I knew I was breaking protocol by going out, but it was that or take the time off, and I needed the money. My supervisor had left it up to me, as I knew the risks.

Well, so I thought I did, which was a fallacy, I found out later. A lot of our work had been at lower elevations, more along streams and rivers, where invasive species would have an easier time getting a hold on things. We would map out what we were finding and also try to eradicate what we could. For larger patches of weeds, a team would come in later and focus on eradication.

But that particular week, I decided to head more into the high country and see how things were doing up at timberline and in the tundra, as we hadn't done much surveying there.

I think, in retrospect, that I was enjoying the solitude and simply wanted a break, as I knew the odds of finding much up there were pretty slim. I was wrong about that, though what I found wasn't necessarily in the realm of botany.

I was backpacking in, and I planned on setting up a base camp, then surveying all around it in concentric circles or grids, depending on the topography, just as we did in the lower areas of the park. But once up in the tundra, all on my own, I started just wandering around, enjoying the stunning beauty of the Northern Rockies. It's a stupendous place—indescribable, really.

Actually, I was almost in Canada, not far from Waterton Lakes National Park. I'd come in that way, as it provided a much easier and closer access to where I wanted to be. I had a tourist boat bring me all the way up the Waterton lakes (there are three, the upper, middle, and lower) and drop me off at Goat Haunt, where I spent my first night in the campground there.

I then hiked along the Waterton River on the Waterton Valley Trail, which is the headwaters for the lakes. Once I got to where Valentine Creek flows into the river, I veered off trail, bushwhacking up the creek and on to where I was under mighty Kootenai Peak. It was stunning country, and I was thoroughly enjoying myself, in spite of the thick alders I had to push through, yet again wondering how I'd managed to get paid to be in such incredible country.

After awhile, I got tired of the bushwhacking and climbed up the slopes of the mountain until I was right at timberline, and there I pitched my little tent on the tundra, not far from tree line.

My first night up there, I saw one of the most beautiful sunsets I've ever seen in my entire life, one I'll never forget, especially since a wolverine came by to see my tent, totally unafraid and more than just a little intimidating. It's said a wolverine can bring down a grown moose, so I kept my distance. It was truly a magical evening, and I felt like I lived a charmed life.

Well, that charm was about to dissipate, unbeknownst to me. I'd been up there for several days, not really doing much except enjoying the rugged beauty and making a half-hearted attempt to look for invasives, when I first heard the cries, and I'll admit, they were unsettling to the point that I immediately considered going back.

I'd been doing this job for several years, basically spending my summers out in various national parks, and I'd never heard anything like them. I wasn't sure what to think. It seemed that my idyllic life had taken a turn towards the sinister.

At first I thought they had to be some kind of distant birds calling in the night, the air currents distorting the sound, then I began to think they were wolves.

Now, my co-worker and I had been in another part of Glacier a few weeks before when we'd heard what sounded like someone hitting a tree with a baseball bat.

It was odd, and we wondered if someone was maybe lost and trying to get attention, until we heard what seemed to be a reply from some distance away, another bat hitting a tree. We decided it was hikers trying to let each other know where they were, and thought no more about it.

What gave me pause was that these cries I was now hearing seemed to be accompanied by more of this thumping sound. I found out later it's called tree knocking, but at the time, it was just plain strange—weird cries and someone whacking a tree over and over. It seemed really odd, especially out in Glacier National Park, one of the quietest and more remote areas in the country.

I'd been basing out of my tent, the tree line only fifty feet or so below me, and I liked being out in the open, as it somehow made me feel safer—you know, bears and all that.

That night, I could hear these sounds far below me, like maybe even way down on Waterton Valley Trail. Even though the cries were about as non-human sounding as could be, I decided it had to be hikers.

I had a light dinner of peanut butter and apples, then made some tea, watched the sun set over the high peaks, then went to bed, tired, thinking of when I should go back out to civilization. Since I was beginning to feel unsettled, I decided the next day would suit me just fine. I could go to Kalispell and regroup and see how my co-worker was doing.

Thinking back on it, it seems that my intuition was telling me something was afoot, even though maybe more on a subconscious level, as I wasn't really scared or anything. We would often stay out a week or more, since packing in was such a chore, and I liked getting as much done as possible while in the outback. But though I'd only been out a few days, I felt like going back, and there was nothing stopping me. I wasn't getting much done, anyway.

I was quickly asleep, tired. I woke early, just in time to watch a small herd of mountain goats make haste right by my tent in the dim light of dawn. They almost seemed as if they were running from something, as they paid me no mind. I wondered if a bear were nearby, and made sure my bear spray was handy.

I could tell from the way the clouds had moved in during the night that a storm was brewing. It made for a stunning sunrise, and I did manage to get a few photos on my little point-and-shoot camera that I used mostly for photographing plants.

Later, looking through those photos, I found I'd taken one that included the tree line, and this photo was about the only thing that made me realize I hadn't gone mad and just dreamed the whole thing.

I will add that I woke with a really uneasy feeling, then decided it was from the storm. But it was way earlier than I'm normally up, the goats waking me.

Well, since a storm was coming in, I sure didn't want to get caught up above timberline in the lightning, so I started packing up my stuff to leave. I had everything packed except my tent, which I tie onto the outside of my pack, when I heard the cries again, but this time they were much closer.

People have asked me to describe them, and it's hard, but they sounded like a mix of a wolf and a loon, yet there was something disturbingly unnatural about them, as if they were being broadcast through speakers or something, as they had a tinny sound and were really loud.

I listened, and I'll be darned if I didn't get the feeling they were triangulating my position. One would call, then another would answer, then the first, and it would have moved 30 or 40 degrees. There were several of them, and as I stood there, mouth open, the cries sounding out sporadically, I realized the 30 and 40 degrees had become 90 and 180, and I was surrounded.

It was a creepy feeling, and I unclipped my bear spray and took off the safety, suddenly wishing I had a gun. I had no idea if these things were animal or human or large birds or something from another planet, the sounds were that unidentifiable.

Suddenly, my adrenaline kicked in, along with the famous flight or fight response. I immediately took off for the timber, angling between the sounds, leaving my somewhat expensive lightweight tent behind.

Maybe I could slip between them before they realized what was going on. It sounded like there were a couple in the trees below and maybe a couple more uphill from me in a rocky outcropping.

I hesitated for a moment, wondering if heading for the timber was the right thing to do, then I ran on, knowing it was my only hope of not being seen. I was soon in the trees, trying to be quick but quiet, making my way downhill toward the bottom of the valley where the creek was. If I could reach it, I knew I could make decent time, then get out to the Waterton Valley Trail and maybe meet up with other hikers.

I had no idea what I was running from, but my instincts said I was in danger. Keep in mind that, even though I'd left my tent behind, I was still carrying a heavy backpack, which was slowing me down, catching on the thick undergrowth and tree limbs.

I estimate I was a good half-mile from the tent when all hell broke loose. I mean, I could hear screaming and howling and carrying on like these things were right there next to me, they were so loud. And I knew they'd found my tent, intending to find me instead, and were now beyond angry. How I knew this I don't know, I just did.

I quickly took my day pack from my larger pack, put some gorp in it, along with my GPS, my maps with my research notes on them, my camera, a water bottle, some matches, and my down coat, then I ditched the big pack and started running. I've never been so terrified in my life, and it's a testament to my survival skills that I was able to think clearly enough to even grab what I did.

I could soon hear the smashing of branches and tree limbs as they came after me, and I knew there was no way I could outrun whatever it was. I still had no idea what was going on, but I felt a deep terror that drove me blindly onward.

I was following a small rivulet, which made the going somewhat easier, as it made somewhat of a path through the thick timber. I could no longer hear the sound of branches breaking, but I knew they were still coming.

As the rivulet widened, I came to a place where a small pool had formed, creating a muddy area full of some kind of tiny bird prints, maybe dippers. I don't know why, unless it was the thought that maybe these were wolves after me, but it occurred to me that I would be wise to try to mask my scent.

I knew many predators have keen senses of smell, so I stopped and began spreading mud all over myself and my pack, head to toe, as thick as possible. I then drank from my water bottle, refilled it, and quickly headed out, though first making sure I hadn't left any tracks that might identify me.

I was dripping with mud, but this was good, as it made me feel like maybe my scent wouldn't be as strong. I knew dogs rolled in carrion as a way to disguise their scent, an old remnant instinct from the days when they were wild.

Now I again heard the cries, but they sounded like they were over to my right, still in the thick timber. Had I somehow lost them? The sound was chilling, to say the least. What were they, and why were they after me?

I finally reached Valentine Creek, where I bushwhacked my way downstream until I finally reached the Waterton Valley Trail. I couldn't believe how quickly I'd come down, as it had taken me hours to get up to where I'd been camped.

I took off jogging back the way I'd come in. The Waterton Valley Trail, like its name indicated, followed along the Waterton River until it came to the ranger station and campground at Goat Haunt.

It was a long ways, and I questioned if I would ever get back, but at least now I knew I wouldn't get lost, and the odds of meeting other hikers had just increased. Safety in numbers and all that, or so I thought.

It was now early afternoon. I was exhausted, but I could think of nothing but getting back to safety. I'd left my car parked in the small town of Waterton, and once there, I could get something to eat and head back to Kalispell, or even get a motel room. But I still had miles to go, and I had no idea if these things were following me or not.

I hadn't heard any cries for some time, not since I'd gotten on the trail. I would need to get a boat at Goat Haunt, or I'd be stuck hiking back a long ways along the shore of Upper Waterton Lake. I wasn't even sure if that particular trail was accessible from Goat Haunt. Upper Waterton Lake is the largest of the three lakes and goes all the way from Glacier National Park into Canada.

I'd no more thought it than I heard a distant cry, which filled me with dread. They weren't that far behind, and they seemed to know which way I was going! I had hoped that being on a somewhat well-used trail would deter these creatures, but I was wrong.

I could no longer jog, as my sides were aching. Even at that, I'd had to stop and rest every few hundred feet, and I'd been so scared I hadn't stopped to eat or drink. I was getting fatigued beyond reason, and I knew I had to stop soon or I would collapse.

I could now see what looked like Upper Waterton Lake, but I couldn't tell what part of the long narrow lake I was seeing through the forest, whether it was near or I was seeing the far shores. For some reason, I thought that maybe when I got to Goat Haunt, I'd be safe, as there are usually a number of people camped there, plus boaters.

I heard another cry, and it was definitely closer. My heart began racing, and without even thinking it through, I diverted off the trail and scrambled down to the Waterton River. I had to stop and take a break. I was totally winded and dying of thirst.

I slid down off the riverbank to the edge of the shallow water. That late in the season, I could easily wade across the river if need be. The mud I'd plastered all over myself was dried and caking off, and I needed a fresh supply to cloak my scent, but I needed food and water and rest even more. But I knew that hiding my scent was of paramount importance, so I quickly again rubbed mud all over myself from head to toe.

Another cry, and now much closer! It sounded so full of hatred, or was I just imagining it? Had I somehow intruded on their territory? Why were they after me?

Now walking along the bank, I spotted a large tree whose roots had been exposed where the bank was eroding away, creating a small hole. I quickly made my way to it, hoping it might provide a place to hide.

It was tight, but I managed to cram myself back into the hole, basically up behind the mass of roots. I felt I was well-hidden, yet I could still see out somewhat. It was dank and claustrophobic feeling, but maybe I could rest here, drink some water and eat some of the gorp in my small pack, then again head back down the trail.

I dearly wanted to get to Goat Haunt before dark, especially since I'd forgotten my headlamp. The idea of spending the night out in the cold and uncertainty wasn't a pleasant one, I can tell you that.

I pulled my down coat from my pack, glad I'd had the presence of mind to stuff it in there. Putting it on, I knew it would help keep me warm if I did have to spend the night, plus its dark green color was good for helping me blend into the riverbank. The only bad thing was that it wasn't covered with mud, and I worried that it carried my scent. I grabbed a handful of dirt and rubbed it on the coat.

I then ate several handfuls of trail mix, emptied my water bottle, and basically passed out from exhaustion. When I woke it was dusk, and I panicked, but then settled down, realizing I was in a good place and would be better off sleeping through the night and starting out when I was rested and it was daylight. Plus, these things would hopefully be long gone by then. They obviously hadn't found me, and it had been a few hours, so maybe they'd gone on back.

I couldn't see them wanting to go near human habitation, where they were likely to get shot. And as I dozed back off, I again wished I had a gun, my bear spray handy.

I awoke in the night, chilly but somewhat rested. I was feeling better, but was getting thirsty again and my water bottle was empty. The river was nearby, but I was too afraid to leave my hiding place so stayed put, and it wasn't long until the gurgling of the water lulled me back to sleep.

I suddenly awoke, terrified, for something with sharp claws was grabbing at my pant leg. I was afraid to move, but in the dim light of dawn I could see a small pair of beady eyes looking up at me.

It was a pine marten! I'd seen these small animals many times in Glacier. They seemed very intelligent and fed on fish, insects, and vegetation. It seemed totally unafraid of me, and sat there as if waiting for something. Maybe I'd invaded its nest, I thought, and it was waiting for me to leave.

It was then that I heard something nearby, something that was making no effort at all to be stealthy and quiet. The marten now crawled up behind me into the hood of my coat, and I knew it was hiding. Whatever was out there, it was more frightened of it than it was of me.

I know bears will eat pine martins when they can catch them, though it was rare, so I suspected it was a bear foraging about. But suddenly a strong smell drifted in, and I knew it wasn't a bear. Bears can smell pretty gnarly, but this thing smelled more like a pit toilet. It was all I could do to not gag, and I slowly put my hands over my nose, trying to break the smell's potency.

I couldn't see much through the tangle of roots, but I definitely smelled something, and my senses were totally overwhelmed to the point that I wanted nothing more than to flee. I began quietly taking deep breaths, trying to still my fears. The little pine marten hidden down in my hood made no movement at all.

It seems like I sat there stiff and cold for an eternity, but I must've gone back to sleep. When I woke, I could see the light glow on the river from the dawn. I could barely move, but I reached up and felt the hood of my coat. The pine marten was gone. This was a good sign.

I listened for the longest time, afraid that whatever had been there was still waiting. Finally, when the sun began to break through the trees and the birds started chirping, I realized that there was probably nothing out there.

It was all I could do to pull myself from behind the root ball, I was so stiff and sore, but I was soon down by the river, filling my water bottle and drinking. At that point, it was a choice between getting giardia and dying of dehydration. I drank several bottles, downed the rest of my gorp, then pulled myself up the bank and back onto the trail.

People asked me later if I found any tracks, which would have helped me identify what was out there, but in all honesty, I was too tired to even think to look. All I cared about was getting to Goat Haunt, and I was so sore from spending the night basically half-standing that it seemed like an iffy proposition to do even that.

But as I stumbled down the trail, I began to loosen up and was soon making pretty good time. The little bit of sunlight that had lit up the river was now just a memory, as the sun was now hidden behind dark and menacing-looking clouds.

I was still wearing my down coat, and I knew the coat would be useless if it got wet, as it wasn't waterproof. My waterproof shell was back in my pack, somewhere above Valentine Creek. I knew I needed to hurry.

It seemed like it took forever, but I finally reached Goat Haunt, to my relief. The campground was empty except for one youngish looking backpacker ready to head up the trail, a single fellow with a pack so big it towered over his head. Keep in mind that it was September, which is nearly winter in the Canadian Rockies. You'll meet day hikers, but rarely do backpackers go out then, as the weather's too iffy, with deep snows not unusual.

When he saw me, he came over to talk, giving me the strangest look and asking if I was OK.

I'd forgotten I was caked in mud and dirt. I wasn't sure what to say —I mean, I could lie and said I'd fallen or something, but could I live with myself if I didn't tell this young guy what had happened? He was alone, and therefore more vulnerable. The park rangers in both Waterton and Glacier always discourage people from going out alone, especially backpacking.

I decided to level with him. I told him why I was caked in mud, where I'd spent the night, and all about the cries and smells and the feeling that I was being hunted.

By the time I'd finished, he'd taken his pack off and leaned it against a tree, looking concerned. When I told him I was a park botanist, that seemed to add the credibility my story needed, and as he hoisted his pack back on, he said he was going out with me.

His name was John, and we got to be friends. He later told me he'd been feeling uncertain about his hike ever since the previous night, as if intuition was telling him not to go, plus the weather looked sketchy. The ranger at the station there had also tried to discourage him.

I can't tell you how happy I was to have someone with me, but the clincher was that even though we wanted to get to Waterton, there was no way to get there. The ranger station was closed, and there was no one else around. We sat there at a picnic table for some time, listening for the sound of a boat motor, but no one came.

After we'd sat there for some time, John grabbed me by the arm. He motioned for me to listen, and there, in the distance, were the cries again. He looked white as a sheet.

I panicked. Where could we go? These creatures seemed to have figured out where I'd gone, for the sounds weren't all that far away.

To our relief, it was then that a park boat came along, a ranger coming out to check on things. He docked the boat and had soon opened the ranger station, where we went inside.

I really don't recall much of what was said, as I was so fatigued and disoriented from a lack of sleep, but I do recall John and I taking the ranger back outside, where we sat for awhile, listening, the ranger looking skeptical.

Sure enough, more cries, and they were even closer, and now the ranger looked worried. He decided it would be prudent for us all to get back to Waterton, especially given the incoming weather. We boarded the boat, and I'll never forget reaching the end of the lower lake, the distant sight of the Prince of Wales Hotel up on the hill above town welcoming us back to civilization.

Once back in Waterton, I got a room and cleaned up as best as I could, trying to rub off all the mud. And even though the ranger we'd met knew my story, I decided to go to the Waterton Lakes National Park offices there and meet with the ranger on duty.

I wanted them to know what had happened for several reasons, but primarily so they would be aware that the pack and tent were mine, in case someone reported a missing person. I didn't have much hope of ever getting them back, for even if no one bothered them, being out all winter would pretty much cause them to deteriorate.

The ranger knew me from my job, so he wasn't as skeptical as I had anticipated. He simply said he'd had other reports from up there, but no one had actually been threatened like I had. He told me he hadn't believed the reports until then, and now he was starting to wonder, but wasn't sure what to do.

I called my supervisor, telling her I was out and that I'd be back at Glacier headquarters the next day and would meet with her. Once there, I told her the exact same story. Like the Waterton ranger, she was skeptical, yet listened. And since it was so close to the end of the season, she said I could finish my plant maps and report and call it a year, which I did.

I spent a few days in Kalispell visiting my co-worker, who was doing well, telling him the story, and I know it scared him to death. Neither of us ever went back to Glacier, instead working the next season down in Texas in Big Bend National Park, then at various other places.

The guy I met at the campground and I stay in touch, and he's told me more than once that I saved his life, though neither of us know what would've actually happened had he gone on. He may have been fine, or maybe the weather would've turned him around before anything happened, as it snowed two feet in Waterton that night. But those cries we heard indicate otherwise.

Strangely enough, someone did find my pack the next spring, and it was pretty much intact. I asked the park service to keep it, for I'd replaced everything in it by then, except for a small hand-held digital recorder that I sometimes used to take notes while in the field. I asked them to send that to me, though I was doubtful it would still work after being out all winter, though it was secure in a waterproof case inside the pack.

When I got it back, I replaced the batteries, and sure enough, it still worked. I listened to my ramblings for awhile, notes to myself about plants and what I was seeing, then it simply went quiet. It was as if the recorder had been on but no one was saying anything. I found that odd, but not really indicative of anything.

But when I was going through my photos later, I found those I'd taken just before abandoning my tent and running away. Most weren't worth keeping, but there was one of the edge of the forest with something that looked odd. I zoomed in and studied it for awhile. What I saw gave me the chills, even though it was indistinct and hard to make out.

There, right along the tree line, looking out at me, was a huge blob-like thing, something very large and very black, and the camera had picked up a glare that looked like it had red eyeshine. There was no way it was a bear, for it had large and very long arms and shoulders that made it look like it could pick up a Volkswagen.

Not long after that, I got a call from the same park ranger at Waterton who'd taken us out by boat. He told me they'd found my tent, and it was ripped to shreds.

I wasn't surprised by this, though it did make the hair on my neck stand up. But when he told me three other hikers had seen several what he called Sasquatch up under Porcupine Ridge on the Boulder Pass Trail, which is near where I'd been camped, I knew I hadn't gone crazy, even though I'd wondered about my sanity since then. They hadn't been approached by the creatures and had immediately left the park.

Would I tell people to *not* backpack in Glacier? No, it's just too beautiful to not see, at least once in one's lifetime, but I would definitely never go alone. But if you do, don't forget my mudpack trick, for I really do think it's what saved my life, as I know it made it harder for them to track me.

But basically, just take my advice and don't go alone.

2

THE RIBBONS IN THE SKY

I met Jessie while waiting in line at a bagel shop in my hometown of Steamboat Springs, Colorado. I was wearing a hat that read, "Bigfoot is Blurry," and I noticed he seemed interested in it.

I jokingly asked him if he believed in Bigfoot, and I must say I wasn't prepared for his answer when he said he'd seen one. He told me he lived down in southwestern Colorado, so I at first figured that's where he'd seen it, and I was really curious, as I've heard some pretty hairy reports from that area. Ironically enough, Jessie ends his story by saying he now lives far from Bigfoot, but I'm not so sure about that.

When I asked him where he'd had an encounter and he said in the Sweet Grass Hills of Montana, I knew I had to talk to him, so I invited him to come fishing with me. I love hearing stories about Montana, but I seldom hear much from the high-grass prairies of the eastern part of that state.

Jessie said he wasn't much of a fisherman, so we took our bagels and sat in the park by the Yampa River, where he told me the following story.
—Rusty

· · ·

My name's Jessie, and there's a little backstory I need to tell so you'll understand why I felt like I did many years later down in Montana. It goes like this:

My dad's sister married a Canadian fellow before I was born. I have no idea how they met, but she ended up moving up to Edmonton and getting her Canadian citizenship, making her a dual citizen.

Well, her husband was a native guy from the Northwest Territories, a Dene, and even though he had a good job there in Edmonton in the oil business, his family ties ran deep, so he managed to get transferred back to where he was from, which was Yellowknife.

So, my aunt's family now lived in one of the more remote areas of Canada, up in the land of lakes and boreal forest and midnight sun—and mosquitoes.

As a kid growing up in Wyoming, Yellowknife might as well have been Antarctica as far as I was concerned, as it seemed just about as far away and remote.

Well, when I was about 10, my grandpa got sick, and my mom went back to Missouri to care for him. My dad was a truck driver and was gone a lot, so my aunt up in Yellowknife offered to have me come up there for awhile.

To me, it sounded like quite an adventure, and I was eager to go. Before I knew it, I was on a plane to Yellowknife, Northwest Territories, a place I'd hardly even known existed until then.

It was a period in my life that I'll never forget, and it helped mold me into the person I am now, as my uncle taught me more about the natural world than I could've ever learned on my own, him being Native and knowing the ways of subsistence living.

My two cousins were about the same age I was, and we got to be pretty good friends. I've kind of lost touch with them, but as far as I know they both still live in Yellowknife.

I was there for the summer and well into the fall, even going to school for awhile. It was long enough to get to know the area pretty well. My aunt's husband was gone quite a bit, but when he came home, he would take me and my two cousins out with him fishing and boating and generally just doing things outside so we didn't drive my aunt crazy.

My uncle's name was Jonas, and like I said, he was part of the Dene people. His family and ancestors had lived in the area for as long as anyone could remember, and they were a pretty traditional bunch. He knew a lot about the Dene way of life, including their folklore and stories, and of course, he wanted his kids to carry on the old traditions. When we were out with him, he would often tell us stories.

The days are long up north, and in the summer they seem like they last forever. But with September, the days grow shorter, and sometimes you can see the Northern Lights. Some people actually go up to view them in September and October because it's not so cold and the lights can be pretty fantastic.

Anyway, one day my uncle and cousins and I were out on his boat on the Great Slave Lake, and it was going on towards dusk. We'd been fishing, and my uncle had kind of let the time get away from him, as we were catching quite a few fish. As an evening breeze began to stir things, he looked kind of serious, realizing that we needed to get back to shore.

Well, at least that's what I thought was his reason for suddenly putting everything away and heading back. In retrospect, I now think it had more to do with the small bands of color we could see to the north as it got darker, bands of yellow and pink.

We finally got back to his truck, put all our gear and the fish in the back, crowded inside, and took off for home. By then, the Aurora was becoming more pronounced, and half the sky was filled with the most beautiful swirling colors I'd ever seen. I was awestruck. It was my first time ever seeing the Northern Lights.

When we got back to Yellowknife, it was dark and the lights were rippling across the entire sky. My aunt and uncle had a pretty nice house with a garage, and I remember my uncle didn't even take the time to unload anything, he just drove straight into the garage, threw the fish into the freezer, and kind of hustled us all into the house. He was usually very methodical about cleaning and putting everything away.

During the night the lights were so strong they actually lit up my room. I remember standing at my window for a long time, watching the ribbons sway, wishing I had a camera and feeling a strong sense of exhilaration.

I knew everyone else was in bed, but I just couldn't tear my eyes from the sight out my window, and I finally decided to go outside where I could see better. Not wanting to wake anyone, I quietly snuck out the kitchen door and into the backyard.

I hadn't been standing there more than five minutes when my uncle came outside, grabbed me by the arm, and gently started pulling me back into the house. It was the only time I ever argued with him, for I held him in great respect, but I wasn't about to go inside and miss seeing one of the most wonderful things I'd ever experienced.

He didn't try to force me, but instead stood there with me, and in retrospect, I have great admiration for what he did, as I now realize how afraid he must've been.

As we stood there, he told me something I'll never forget.

"The ribbons in the air are the spirits of people who have passed in a bad way, Jessie. When you look up at them, you're inviting them to enter your life. And sometimes when you look up it looks like a circle, which is the spirits holding hands and dancing. The Tlingit people believe this also."

All the while he was talking, he refused to look up, even though I was still enthralled and had my eyes to the sky.

He continued. "If they come down low, you must get inside, for you can inhale them and they'll kill you. And whatever you do, don't whistle, for that draws them closer. But we should go inside now, for the lights also draw the Wendigo, and they are very bad."

With that, he again gently pulled on my arm, and I decided it was time to go inside. He didn't actually use the word Wendigo, but instead used a Dene word which I've half-forgotten, but I think it sounded kind of like *Wechuge*.

Once back inside, he asked me not to go back out, which I agreed to. He then said, "There's more to the lights than we'll ever know. Once, when out with my grandfather, we actually heard the lights. They whistled, then made a crackling sound. And it was then we saw the Wendigo. Jessie, it's real, we actually saw it, and it started towards us, but my grandfather had a rifle and shot into the air and it turned and went away. I know you'll soon be back home, where you can't see the lights, but I've heard the Wendigo travels far, so take care and don't go out alone at night in the wilds, especially near lakes, for they love the water."

With that, I went back to my room, where I have to admit I stood for a good hour longer watching the lights, thinking that he was just superstitious. The Northern Lights were just particles—electrons and protons—shot out from the sun that lit up the sky when they collided with the Earth's atmosphere.

OK, let's fast forward about 25 years and to northern Montana, just northeast of Shelby near the Sweet Grass Hills where I was working on a ranch in the tall-grass prairie for a fellow named Jeff. There are few trees in this country, mostly just the windbreaks planted to shelter the ranch buildings.

I was in my mid-thirties and still not married, kind of a drifter, never staying any one place very long. My mom worried about me, but my dad said it was just the trucker genes I'd inherited from him, a form of wanderlust that I'd get over eventually and settle down. By then, I'd been plenty of places and worked both as a ranch hand and in the oil and gas fields, which there are plenty of in that part of Montana. I loved being outdoors and alone.

You know, Rusty, this is kind of an aside, but I read an article about a woman who'd grown up back East on some remote seashore and had wandered around all by herself in nature as a child. She said she'd been incredibly lonely, and she'd eventually grown up and left the area, getting married and having kids and living in a more urban area. But she felt that the best times of her life had been when she was alone as a kid and felt that self-awareness that loneliness brings.

I felt the same way, for I never felt as alive as when I was out in the wilds alone, even if the so-called wilds were just ranch lands or oil fields. But my dad was right, for I eventually did settle down, though it took a few years.

Anyway, so there I was, out in the Sweet Grass, working on an old windmill that had broken down. It was late winter, and just like that time we were out on the Great Slave Lake, I let the darkness overcome me, as I'd been so focused on getting the darn thing fixed. I didn't want to have to go back out there again, as it was bitter cold.

The Sweet Grass Hills are actually several tall buttes that have a bunch of small creeks and coulees coming off them, as they're a good 3,000 feet higher than the surrounding countryside. The coulees provide plenty of places to hide, and after dark, the area can be a bit spooky. I was on an ATV, and I'd almost got stuck a couple of times coming in. It was cold, but there hadn't been much snow that winter.

I was gathering up my tools, wishing I'd headed out before dark, when I heard a whistling sound. Now, this wasn't like someone whistling for their dog, but was much higher pitched and seemed like it was coming from way up high, like maybe something up in the atmosphere.

I was puzzled by this until I saw some bands of color across the sky, just like that night long ago up in Yellowknife when I'd seen the Northern Lights for the first time.

Sure enough, it wasn't long before colorful ribbons were draped across the sky, dancing up and down all over the place, lighting what little snow there was in shades of green and gold and purple. It was amazing, for the lights typically aren't very visible that far south.

Once again, I was awed, wished I had a camera, and felt an incredible sense of exhilaration. But as I stood there, I finally realized the temperature was dropping fast and I needed to get going before I got chilled.

I was dressed warm and had some survival gear with me, which everyone who worked outdoors in the winter in that country carried. I also knew that my boss, Jeff, would notice if I hadn't come back in a reasonable time and would start looking for me, as everyone looked out for one another from necessity. It was just too easy to die out in the Sweet Grass in the winter.

I finally got on my ATV and was ready to start it up when I heard another whistle, only this one sounded like it was coming from a coulee not too far away. And just about then, I had a really weird experience, something I've never had before or since. It actually almost felt mystical, though I'm not superstitious.

I could hear a soft swooshing noise, and it then felt like I was surrounded, like the lights had set down on the landscape all around me. I felt like I was cradled in a soft light, like some giant being had its arms around me.

It had been years since I'd seen the lights back in Yellowknife, and I hadn't given what my uncle had said the merest thought afterwards, but it suddenly all came back to me as if it was only yesterday.

"If they come down low, you must get inside, for you can inhale them and they'll kill you. The lights also draw the Wendigo, and they are very bad."

But before I had time to really process what was happening, a crackling noise began which totally enveloped me. I recalled the rest of what my uncle had said.

"Once, we actually heard the lights. They whistled, then made a crackling sound. And it was then we saw the Wendigo."

Somehow, it seemed as if the particles that caused the lights had touched Earth, with me right in the middle of it all. Yet I felt no great concern, like I was about to die or anything. It just seemed incredibly magical—and very unexpected. I didn't feel like I would die if I breathed it in.

But what happened next was just plain weird. All of a sudden, I could smell cotton candy, and it wasn't a vague odor, but was really strong. And just then, the lights lifted, and I realized I couldn't see anything. It was almost dark, but even my ATV, which was right under me, was cloaked by a colorful fog.

I quickly realized that I was smelling the odor of oil being pumped from the ground, the smell you sometimes get when near pump jacks. There were plenty of those in the Sweet Grass, but none nearby, so I guessed the smell was coming on the breeze. To this day, I'm not sure what was going on, it was so odd to smell something so strong like that with the nearest pump not really all that close.

Now I heard the whistle again, the one coming from a nearby coulee. I was already suspecting what it was, though I refused to believe it. I decided it was a large squirrel and the breeze was amplifying the sound, which in hindsight is ludicrous.

My uncle's words again came back to me: "It was then we saw the Wendigo."

I don't know much about the Wendigo, except it's a legend in the northern parts, but I do know what a Bigfoot's supposed to be, and a part of me said they're either the same thing or very closely related. I, of course, believed in neither, being a pragmatic kind of guy.

As the Northern Lights receded, the fog lifted, and the darkness closed in. I have no idea how long I'd been there watching, but it must've been a lot longer than I'd thought, for it was now pitch dark, and I was getting chilled from the wet fog.

But getting chilled was a lesser worry, for I was suddenly overcome with a deadly fear. My lungs started burning, and it hurt so badly I wasn't sure if I could breathe much longer. Had the lights poisoned me? If so, I was sure it had a logical explanation, maybe something to do with charged particles—or maybe it was from the sweet smell of oil. I had no time to speculate, I just needed to get back.

I started my ATV just as I again heard a whistle, though this time much closer. I could feel myself begin to panic, and it was all I could do to slow my thinking down.

Interestingly enough, I'd just had a conversation a few days before with a friend who'd been through a lot and had discovered a meditation technique she said was helping her. It was simple—you just concentrated on your breathing and nothing else.

I've never had a panic attack, and I knew having one would totally incapacitate me, the opposite of what I needed right then. It seemed to me that my very survival was on the line, then and there. That night must've brought out the philosopher in me, because ever since then I think every so often about how short life is and how quickly our circumstances can change.

I sat there and breathed slowly, in and out, over and over, until the burning lessened and I was able to head my ATV back down the dim road, my headlights barely lighting the way. Fortunately, most of the snow had melted, making the road easy to follow.

It didn't take long for my lungs to clear and the odor to fade away. I was feeling much better and was making good time, almost home, kicking myself for staying out so late, as the wind was now picking up.

The Sweet Grass Hills are notorious for their high winds, mostly because they're at a higher altitude than the surrounding prairie. Thinking about this later, I realized what good habitat they are, as they're fairly extensive, running for about 50 miles east to west. Trees are found here and there on the buttes themselves, but generally the whole area is just tall grass, serving as habitat for lots of deer and animals.

And habitat for something that whistles, I thought warily, finally reaching the ranch house. I stopped and said hello to Jeff and his wife Clara so they would know I was back, then headed for my small trailer.

It was great to be back inside where it was nice and warm, though by then the trailer was beginning to be battered by the wind, which had quickly picked up. I could now feel a draft coming in under the front door, and I rolled up a towel and put it there, then started making myself some dinner.

It wasn't long before the little 22-foot trailer began really rocking, which to be honest, scared me, even though it was tied down. It was the beginning of a big blizzard, and I've often wondered if the incoming storm and the Northern Lights might have somehow created just the right conditions to account for what I'd seen and heard.

But as for the whistle and the strange odor, I knew that was something different, and the more I thought about it, the creepier it got. Keep in mind that this part of Montana is basically right on the Canadian border, and right across that border is Writing on Stone Provincial Park. I'd never visited it, but I had seen photos of some of the petroglyphs there, and one looked just like I imagined the Wendigo to look—big and bulky and scary as heck.

My main job on the ranch was to feed the cattle, and though we had them in a pasture up by the ranch buildings, it could still be a chore, especially in a blizzard.

We had ropes tied between the barn and houses so if visibility got poor we could still find our way around. There was more than one sad story in that country of ranchers getting turned around in blizzards and freezing to death just mere feet from their doors, not knowing where they were.

It was a big barn, pretty historic looking, with a huge hay shed next to it. There had been times when the cattle would get disoriented and lost out in the pasture, dying like those lost ranchers, so when a big blizzard came up, we generally ran them into the inside corrals by the barn, with the barn door open so they could go inside.

There was only about 20 head that winter, as the rest had been sold in the fall. Jeff always shipped his horses down to his brother's place near Billings each winter, which had a somewhat milder climate and more protection from the elements.

That storm raged on, and it was all I could do to force myself out in it to feed, twice a day, even though Jeff would sometimes come out to help. Even his faithful Border Collie, Patches, who normally followed him around, wouldn't budge from the house.

By dawn on the second day, we found that all the cattle were out in the corrals, whereas before they'd been smart enough to stay in the barn, especially since we'd been feeding them inside. But now they were out and acted like they were nervous about something.

Jeff and I tried to haze them into the barn, but none of them would budge. One cow was already down, a white lump in the corral, covered with drifted snow. We managed to get her back on her feet, but she wouldn't go inside.

OK, cattle aren't dumb, and Jeff and I knew there was a reason they wouldn't go in. Had a wolf strayed down from Canada and taken refuge there? We had no choice but to go check it out.

The inside of the barn smelled unusually musty, but we found nothing there. We even went to the hay shed and looked around the stacks of hay, but there was nothing unusual there, either.

Finally, we went ahead and fed in the barn, and lo and behold, the cattle went inside. Jeff decided to shut the door and block them in there, as he didn't want to lose any in the blizzard.

We went back to our respective homes, glad the chores were done. Jeff had a weather radio that had said the storm should end in another day. We'd already got at least two feet of snow, but the winds were piling drifts clear up to the windows of his house. My little trailer was near the hay shed, which provided enough of a break that I didn't get drifted in.

That night the storm raged even more than before, leaving me feeling alone and isolated. I said I like being alone, but that was one time I didn't, for I kept hearing what sounded like a howling above the constant moaning of the wind. It made me uneasy, and I ended up sleeping in my clothes in my recliner, ready in case something happened.

The next morning I woke with a stiff neck, and I immediately felt that something was wrong. It took me awhile, but I realized the wind had quit moaning, the light coming in through the windows was much brighter, and the house felt warm with no drafts. I knew the storm was over.

I bundled up and was soon outside, shoveling a path from my trailer to my pickup, then starting it to be sure the battery wasn't dead. I then made my way to the barn and corrals, and it was then that I had a sinking feeling.

It was barely dawn, but I could see well enough, and it appeared that we'd missed a cow when we'd hazed them into the barn. There in the corral was a big lump, all drifted over and packed with snow.

I felt bad. It was hard enough financially to lose the cow and her unborn calf, as the cows had all been bred that fall, but I felt bad knowing she'd suffered. At least freezing to death was a pretty quick way to die, I consoled myself, grabbing a shovel.

But then something happened that took my breath away. The cow moved! She wasn't dead after all! Maybe the snow had provided enough insulation that she'd been protected from the harsh winds.

It was then that I heard a whistle, just like the one I'd heard in the coulee by the windmill. And then another seemed to answer. The first seemed to be over behind the hay shed, and the second was around the far side of the barn. And I could now hear the cattle all mooing and carrying on, and I knew they were unsettled.

I knew I needed to help the cow get out and up on her feet, but I also knew something strange was going on, and I was suddenly afraid. All I could think of was getting over to the ranch house where Jeff and Clara were. If nothing else, I needed help with the cow.

I headed out, trying to run through the deep snow, which was, of course, impossible. I again heard a whistle, and it was then that something compelled me to turn around and look back.

The cow was getting up, but it wasn't a cow after all! My mind couldn't process what I was seeing, so I at first thought it was a bull, it was so large. But Jeff didn't have any bulls, he always bred the cows through A.I. So what was a bull doing in the corral, and how did it get there?

The "bull" stood and shook itself, whistled towards the hay shed, then walked away as if nothing unusual at all was going on. It acted as if I wasn't even there.

I saw only its backside, but it must've weighed a good 800 pounds. I was pretty familiar with what animals weighed, being in the cattle business. But what really got to me was the fact that it was walking on two feet, taking strides like a human, though covered with thick black hair that flowed like a cape down along its sides. And those arms! Way too long for a human.

I knew then and there I was looking at the creature my uncle had told me about, the Wendigo. And it had to have at least two companions nearby, from the sound of the whistles.

I turned and ran to the house, pounding on the door until Jeff let me inside. By then, the creatures were gone.

I made a hasty decision to keep what I'd seen to myself. Jeff had lived there all his life, and he undoubtedly knew what the Sweet Grass harbored. He may have seen them himself. It wasn't my deal to tell him something he probably already knew, and if he didn't know about them, well, they'd done no harm, so why stir things up?

I made up a lame excuse that I was out of coffee, and he good-naturedly put the pot on, his wife now making breakfast. After eating, I made my decision right then and there to leave. I knew I'd be leaving them in a hard spot, but it was almost spring, and surely they could find someone else to help out. There weren't enough cattle that he couldn't feed them alone, and hopefully he and his wife could do the calving.

I told Jeff I had to leave for a family emergency and would be going as soon as I fed the cows. I could pack up my stuff and be gone in a half-hour, as I've always traveled light. Jeff said he was disappointed, but he understood, and maybe his neighbor would help him out for awhile.

That made me feel better, as I hated lying to him like that, but I knew I couldn't stay even one more night. The sound of that howling above the wind still gives me chills when I think about it.

After breakfast and saying my goodbyes, Jeff cut me a check for work owed, then I went over to the barn to feed one last time. I told Jeff I would do it alone, he could take a break, but in reality, I wanted to go look at the spot where the Wendigo had been.

It looked like a snow cave of sorts, though shallow. I wondered if the creature had been sheltering in the barn and had left before we came to feed. When it came back and found everything locked up, it had huddled down, resorting to its natural defenses and long coat to keep it warm.

I suspected it wasn't the first time it had slept in a snow bank. Its two buddies had probably slept in the lee of the hay shed, out of the wind, but with the whiteout, it may not have been able to find them.

I let the cattle out, and the look on their faces was priceless, as if they hadn't expected the sun to be out. They were soon romping around the corral, but they wouldn't go near the snow bank. I fed them outside for the first time in days, and I made sure to put some of the hay where the snow bank was, as I wanted them to stomp it all away. I didn't want Jeff to know. He and his wife had to stay there, and I just didn't want to worry them.

I was soon gone, half plowing my way with my pickup bumper down the drifted-over roads, almost getting stuck several times before I got to the highway where the snow plows had been busy. I stopped in the nearest town and gassed up, then headed south, far from the Wendigo, or so I hoped.

I spent the rest of the winter in Arizona, where, surrounded by the saguaro and mesquite, everything that had happened seemed like a dream. I finally ended up getting a job at a hardware store in Yuma, probably a reaction to the fears I'd felt there in the Sweet Grass, as it felt nice and safe being in that store.

But as I gradually got over it all, I missed the outdoors and found a job ranching again. I ended up marrying my boss's daughter, just like in the movies, but we live in southern Colorado, far from the Wendigo, as well as the ribbons of light in the sky.

And though I know they're far away in distance, sometimes they're just a little too close in my mind's memory.

3
DOWN AND OUT

This story came from one of my fishing clients. I had about a half-dozen guys on that trip, and we were staying on the edge of the Selway-Bitterroot Wilderness at an old resort that consisted of a number of well-seasoned cabins, which we'd rented for a week of fishing.

The Selway-Bitterroot Wilderness is to the west of the small town of Hamilton and is wild and rugged country. Every year there are reports about hunters and hikers getting lost in what's one of Montana's most pristine wilderness areas, deep in the heart of the Bitterroot Mountains, whose high points define the state line between Montana and Idaho.

I've always felt a bit on edge when in that particular area, and I seldom take people there anymore. It seems that every time I'm in that country I have something strange happen. This trip, I was down at the creek washing the pans when I heard a strange and very unsettling howl come from the distance, and all the guys expressed unsettled feelings of being watched at various times. The area we'd been fishing in has thick forests and lots of creeks—all perfect Bigfoot habitat.

We'd just finished one of my Dutch-oven dinners and were all sitting around the fire, comfortably tired after a good day of fishing. My trips are all catch and release, so instead of trout we had a nice dinner of corn on the cob, biscuits, barbecue beef, and apple cobbler.

After awhile, the talk turned to the many mysteries of the universe, as campfire talk often does, and one of my clients, a fellow I'll call Matt, told us the following story. —Rusty

R usty, my name is Matt, and I'd like to tell you about something that happened probably 30 or more years ago. It still pretty much creeps me out, and to be honest, I really don't like talking about it, but here goes.

I was born and raised in eastern Montana, and since I'm kind of an old guy now, I can remember how things were before there were many people around, though Montana's still pretty uninhabited compared to most states. Where this happened is actually still pretty wild, and I think it's because it's fairly remote and there aren't many roads.

At the time, I was living in the little town of Darby, which now serves as a center for outdoor recreation, mostly fishing. I don't recall the population back then, but it was probably fewer than a hundred. The town sits in a beautiful valley by the Bitterroot River, near some big mountains, like Trapper's Peak.

It used to bother me living there, as I was used to seeing big vistas, not the sides of nearby mountains, as I grew up in the open country of wheat fields. I used to get a bit claustrophobic there, but not nearly as much as after this happened.

You could literally walk a few hundred yards out of town and be in wilderness at that time. There are a lot more houses there now, but it's still pretty much surrounded by the wilds, and I mean for a hundred miles or more in pretty much every direction. And most of it's forested with some deep canyons. There's plenty of room out there for creatures that we don't normally think much about—actually, creatures I prefer to never think about.

I've read a number of your stories where the people involved ended up moving away or decided to never go into the backcountry again, and after this happened, I can say I understand why. I did end up going into the mountains a few times after this, but I never would go alone—or unarmed.

Okay, back to the story. My cousin had a towing business in Hamilton, some distance up the road from Darby, and I worked for him for a few years. My wife eventually got sick and tired of the Montana winters, so we ended up moving out to California where she had family. I sure didn't miss that backcountry after we left, but California back then was pretty nice, not crowded. We live in New Mexico now.

I guess what happened kind of took my enjoyment of nature away, because I used to like going out into the woods and fishing. Now that I'm retired, I'm trying to rekindle some of that enjoyment, which is what led me to sign up for one of your guided trips while visiting family here.

Well, it was winter, and we'd just got a ton of snow, which is always good for the towing business. A lot of times the snows would come through and the roads would get bad, but it usually melted off pretty fast. Well, this time it stayed cold, and the roads were solid ice. Like I said, lots of work for the towing biz.

It was late afternoon, and I'd already rescued a couple of vehicles when my cousin called and sent me up a road not too far out of town that went a few miles up into the wilderness. It followed a creek as far as it could until the canyon got too tight, and then it dead-ended in a small turnaround. Not far from the end of the road were some pretty impressive cliffs. In retrospect, once you get up out of the valley, it always had kind of a forbidding feel to me.

The road was narrow and gradually climbed up the side of the valley until there was a pretty good embankment going down into the creek. I think at one time the road went to an old mine, but it now served as an access road for the few small ranches in the valley.

I'd been told the vehicle was at the turnaround and the owner couldn't get it started. I didn't ask what this person was doing up there in the first place. All I can say is, as a tow-truck driver I'd seen it all, people going places they had no business going in unbelievable conditions with inadequate vehicles and bald tires and half-dead batteries, totally unprepared.

It took awhile to get up there, as the road gradually climbed just enough to make it tricky when iced up. I wanted to stop and put on chains, but there was no place to pull over, and I was afraid if I stopped I'd start sliding backwards or sideways and end up stuck, or worse yet, off the side. It was like trying to steer a toboggan.

I finally made it up to the turnaround where, sure enough, there sat a little white Honda. A guy who looked to be in his 50's was standing next to it, looking sheepish and glad to see me, as it was bone-chilling cold.

He appeared to be dressed warm enough, but he had two dogs with him, a couple of short-haired hounds, and he asked if I would put them in my truck where it was warm. They were both shivering, and I felt a bit of irritation that this guy would endanger his dogs by taking them up there in the first place, but I said nothing and just put them in the truck cab, which was nice and warm.

The car was fairly close to the edge of the road, and he said he was worried about getting stuck, wanting me to follow him out after we got the car started.

I knew if he did go off even a little, I would never be able to pull him back on the road without chains, so I took some time and put my chains on, which was kind of a pain, as it was so cold.

I later asked my wife how cold it had been down in town, and she said the thermometer had read 15 degrees, and I know it was way colder up there, as the wind was blowing. My wife was kind of a weather geek when we lived in Montana, as she loved torturing me about how cold it was there and how nice it was in California. Once we moved back there, she never looked at another thermometer, as far as I know.

Chains on, I managed to turn around in the tight spot to where I could get in front and give him a jump. We didn't have those portable starter jumpers they have now. But for some reason the car wouldn't start, and I was then beginning to think it wasn't the battery, even though nothing would turn on, no lights or anything. I was beginning to think something else was wrong.

It was now early evening, and the cold was intensifying enough that I was starting to get chilled, even though I was dressed warm. The wind had finally died down, and I could see frost crystals in the air. I knew it was going to be a bitterly cold night.

Finally, I radioed my cousin for ideas, but he was a good 30 miles away working on another rescue and couldn't help. I was thinking maybe I'd just tow the guy to a shop where they could check it out, though it was so slick and icy I wasn't real keen on pulling him down that hill. It was one of the few times in my towing career that I finally had to admit defeat.

I told the customer that we had no choice but to go back down and come back tomorrow. He could get a motel, and I'd pick him up in the morning, and we'd go try again and tow him out if need be.

He looked upset and refused to go with me. I was shocked, as it seemed suicidal to me to stay out there in the cold—even if he could deal with it, I was doubtful his dogs could. His car had Minnesota plates, so I figured he at least knew something about the cold, but you just can't stay warm in a car without the engine and heater running.

He then informed me that he had a warm sleeping bag and a small propane space heater for his car and would be fine, and tomorrow he'd call again if he still needed help. After some hesitation, he asked if I'd mind taking his dogs for the night, as he didn't want anything to happen to them.

I told him that was fine, though I somehow suspected there was something else going on. What was he doing out here in the first place? It just seemed like there was more to his story than he was wanting to say.

So, I drove off into the dark, glad for the chains, as going downhill was even more treacherous. His dogs were there in the cab with me, and as I drove off, I told him I'd come back tomorrow and bring the dogs back. He seemed really appreciative, but wouldn't budge on coming with me.

Back home, I called my cousin Ed, who decided to call the local sheriff, Jim, a good friend of his, and tell him about the situation. I was happy to hear this, for I knew Jim would go up there with a backup deputy or two and hopefully persuade the guy to come out for the night.

Maggie, my wife, took the dogs in and fed them, then we made them a nice bed in the living room by the fireplace, where they settled down for the night, looking very appreciative.

At that time we still had Boggs, our old Cocker Spaniel, and I think he was pretty pleased, thinking he was having a sleepover, as he actually ended up sleeping out there with them instead of on top of my feet like he usually did, which was fine by me. Boggs died a few years later at the ripe old age of 15, and I still miss him.

So anyway, Ed called me a few hours later to inform me that Sheriff Jim and his crew had gone up there, but there was no sign of a car stuck at the turnaround. Funny thing was, it had snowed a little since I'd left, and there was no sign of any tracks coming out, either.

But what they did find was a bit chilling and left me with a strange feeling. They said when they got there and were looking around, they were somewhat surprised to find several sets of huge footprints going on up towards the cliffs in the deep snow.

They at first thought they might belong to the guy with the stuck car, but it didn't take long to realize the stride was way too long and the tracks too deep, plus why so many? It pretty much creeped them out, and after being pretty sure there was no car anywhere around, they left.

Now, let me add a little backstory here. The autumn before all this happened, several hunters had gone missing up there, and they'd eventually been found, but the story they told when they came out was pretty incredible. I don't remember all the details, but I do recall they'd been accosted by a strange creature that was big and black, probably what we now call a Bigfoot, though back then sightings were more rare. I personally think Bigfoot have always been around, but there just weren't as many people so they weren't seen very often.

I can't recall for sure, but I think they called it a big hairy monster, which I found kind of funny, like something a kid would make up.

I've been told that the natives that once lived in that area also had legends about seeing Bigfoot, but I always laughed and wrote it off to overactive imaginations. After all, I'd spent my childhood wandering around the countryside, though admittedly not the mountains. The whole idea was nonsense to me.

So, when Ed told me all this, I did pause a little, but after talking to Maggie, we decided the customer had walked around, leaving footprints, then somehow got his car started and driven out before the new snow and therefore didn't leave any car tracks.

Usually when snow melts tracks will get larger, so I figured that was what was going on, though I knew it had been getting colder, not warmer. But sometimes the mind grabs onto whatever it can when confronted with strange things.

But if Sheriff Jim and his guys had said the tracks were too deep and rangy for a human, who was I to question their assessment? These guys were sensible and pragmatic and not at all prone to drama.

But I had a heck of a time sleeping that night. The fellow had my number, so if he'd come out, why hadn't he arranged to get his dogs? Maybe it was late and he knew they'd be fine with me, and he'd call in the morning.

Surely the guy had somehow gotten his car started, but was there some connection with the tracks? Was he still somehow up there? My mind just wouldn't stop racing.

Finally, around six a.m., I got up and made a pot of coffee. I let the dogs out in the yard while it was brewing, then fed them all an early breakfast and sat in the living room, not wanting to wake Maggie.

Boggs and one of the hounds got into playing tug of war on a pull toy and I had to shut that down, as they were too noisy. The hounds seemed pretty happy, but maybe they always acted like that.

It was starting to get daylight, and I could see that the storm had passed and it would be a nice sunny day. Part of me wanted to get out and drive back up to where the car had been stuck, but the other part wanted to stay where it was warm—and safe.

Safe? Was I actually just a little afraid of a mythological creature?

I laughed at myself, then finally made some breakfast, just as Maggie was stirring.

Maggie and I have always been close, and as we sat there at the kitchen table, I told her everything I was feeling. She didn't bat an eye, saying it was all superstition, but she also told me she didn't want me going back up there alone. In fact, if the sheriff hadn't found anything, why should I even feel obliged to go back at all? She assured me that the fellow was probably out and would eventually call about the dogs.

I tried to relax, but I just couldn't forget about this guy. You might say I was worried about getting stuck with his hounds, but that wasn't it at all. In retrospect, some sixth sense was telling me that if it were me, I would want someone to come back and figure out what was going on. Of course, if it were me, I wouldn't have gone out there in the first place.

I guess I wasn't the only one thinking about this, as Ed called, saying he and Jim were going back up there and they wanted me to come along and show them exactly where the car had been.

I was soon following them in my tow truck, chains still on, though things were starting to warm up. It was still slick, though, and we had to take our time getting up there. Once there, I walked over and looked at the strange tracks while the others were looking for any clues as to where the car had gone.

The tracks had gone to the base of the cliffs, then just disappeared, as if scaling them. And I could clearly see that my hypothesis about the melting snow making them larger was wrong, as nothing had melted. So much for trying to rationalize things. The tracks were huge, and it was obvious that whatever had made them had two feet, not four, like a bear. I know Sheriff Jim took photos, and I wish I'd done the same.

Well, we all walked around and tried to figure out where the car had gone, and once I looked over the edge, it was pretty obvious. There it sat, at the bottom of the embankment, and it looked pretty smashed up.

We stood around for a minute, trying to figure out what had

happened. You might say it was obvious, the guy had somehow got his car started and then slid over the edge, but it wasn't that simple.

We could see where the car had been, as there were tracks all over the place from everyone the night before, but there were no tire tracks going off the edge. This was why the guys hadn't seen it the night before—there was virtually nothing obvious to indicate it had gone over the side.

Instead of tire tracks, there was a place where it appeared something had been pushed over the side, which wasn't as visible the night before in the dark, but was now more apparent.

Being a little better dressed than Ed and Jim, I volunteered to go over the side and check things out, dragging the tow cable alongside me. I was wearing my heavy snowmobile suit and boots, having gotten cold the previous night. The embankment wasn't so steep that I couldn't slide down it, though the snow was fairly deep, and I made my way down, holding onto branches and bushes along the way.

Once at the bottom, I dreaded looking inside the car, for I was pretty sure I'd see the fellow from the night before, but there was nobody, much to my relief. But I just couldn't believe what I was seeing—the car looked like it had been pushed sideways over the edge, no easy task.

I got on my radio and asked Ed to verify what I was seeing, and he said he and Jim both thought it was odd. I then told him I was going to hook up so they could pull the car out, as there was nobody inside.

It was a pretty standard recovery, and I watched them winch the car from above as I stood below, waiting for the coast to be clear before I climbed back up. And while I stood there, watching the car slowly being pulled up the slope, I got a very strong feeling that something was watching me.

It was so ominous that I turned around and scanned everything behind me, trying to overcome the urge to flee, feeling that my life was in danger.

I didn't see a thing, but I can tell you I was up that slope in half the time it took me to come down, which is the opposite of what you'd expect.

Sheriff Jim searched the car and found nothing unusual, just the guy's sleeping bag and normal personal stuff, like clothes and such. He took the guy's registration papers from the glove box—he would use these to figure out who he was and contact his family. So far, he was considered a missing person, though for all we knew he'd walked down into town and was having himself a big breakfast at the diner. The registration said his name was Miles.

Well, we towed the car on in and that was that, we were all soon on to other things. I had a recovery where someone had slid off into the borrow pit, just the normal busy kind of day, and it wasn't until evening that I was able to get home and see how Maggie and the dogs were all doing.

Ed called and hadn't heard a word from the dogs' owner, Miles, though he said Sheriff Jim had managed to track down the guy's daughter, though she hadn't heard anything from her dad. They all lived in some little town in Minnesota.

The hounds seemed happy enough, but it was another sleepless night for me. I just couldn't understand how the car had been pushed sideways off the edge, and I kept flashing back to that ominous feeling. What if the guy had been the victim of some kind of foul play—foul play by creatures I didn't even believe in?

Maggie finally got tired of my tossing and turning and went and slept in the spare bedroom.

Now, what I'm about to relate here should be taken in the context that I'm not a bit superstitious—I don't even believe in ghosts, so you can bet I was as shocked as anyone could be over all this.

It started with the two hounds and Boggs trying to get in bed with me. Now, like I said, Boggs usually sleeps on top of the covers at my feet, but he was actually trying to get under the covers, which he'd never once in his life tried to do. He had that long Cocker Spaniel coat and slept pretty warm, no need for covers.

The hounds were doing the same, so I wondered if the fire hadn't gone out. I got up to check, but no, it was fine. I put a few more logs on, and as I was sitting there kind of poking at it, I thought I heard something outside.

Now, all of a sudden, I had that ominous feeling again, like I was being watched by someone or something that meant me harm. And given that the dogs were also hiding, I knew it wasn't my imagination.

I went to my gun cabinet and unlocked it, taking out my shotgun and loading it. I had no idea what was going on, but I wasn't going to just sit around unprepared.

Just like that, the feeling lifted, and I knew something had been watching me—something that maybe understood what a gun was for.

Maggie is much more security minded than I am, and she always makes sure the curtains are pulled at night, but as I walked around, I could see where they'd been pulled back at the big living-room picture window, enough that someone could easily see inside. I wondered if one of the hounds hadn't done it, trying to see outside, and I closed it back up.

I was too afraid to go outside until dawn, but when I did, I was dumbfounded to find tracks—giant tracks, about the same size as those up in the snow. I took photos and went back inside, now very much on edge.

I wasn't sure whether I should show the tracks to Maggie or not, but decided I'd better so she would be on guard. Her reaction wasn't good, is all I can say, as I'd told her all about the tracks up the road. She decided they'd somehow followed me home, which wouldn't be all that hard to do, given the condition of the roads and how slow I was going.

Maggie was the first to actually use the term Bigfoot, but I'd suspected all along that's what was going on. My skepticism was losing out to the facts, is all I can say, but I still didn't want to believe this was what it was. I told her we'd been pranked, but I knew better, given the dogs and the strange feeling of being watched. I just didn't want to admit things like this could exist.

She made breakfast while I tried to persuade the dogs to go outside, which they were reluctant to do. I was now wondering if we were going to end up with the hounds, as I knew Maggie would never take them to the shelter, providing the guy never showed up to claim them.

She'd actually named them, and I felt this was a bad portent, as we didn't need more dogs, especially hounds, as they're hard to keep from running. Boggs always stayed with us when we took him for walks.

But the hounds were the least of my problems right then. I just couldn't get out of my head that I needed to go back up again and look for the guy. I barely even knew his name, for crying out loud, and he'd said he didn't want a ride, so why should I worry?

I don't know the answer to that, except to say I wouldn't want people to give up on me easily if I were lost—assuming he was.

Maggie refused to let me go back up there alone, and Ed and Jim were both busy, so she finally agreed to come along. We'd take our Jeep and lots of warm clothes and survival gear and leave the dogs at home. I also took my radio so I could call Ed if needed. And I was sure to pack my shotgun and plenty of ammo.

What I didn't know at the time was that taking Maggie along would save my life—or at least that's how it seemed.

It didn't take us long to get up there, as the roads had pretty much melted off and were muddy, but not too bad. Once there, I showed Maggie what was left of the tracks, though they'd melted down a bunch and were hard to make out.

She didn't say a word—she didn't need to, as the look on her face said it all.

Well, there we were, and I had no idea what to do next. There was no way we could climb those cliffs to go on a search, nor did we want to do something so foolhardy. I decided to take one last look around to set my mind at ease, and we did just that, walked around and looked. We found nothing unusual.

But we did hear something. Far in the distance, from way above in the wilds of the Bitterroots, came a sound that chilled us both to the very bone. And even though it was broad daylight, we both had that sense of foreboding one gets when out in the dark alone and vulnerable.

We stood there for a moment, listening to the strangest call ever, a sound that came from massive lungs and went on and on like a siren until it disintegrated into a low bellow like a bull. We weren't prepared for anything like that, but when the call was answered from somewhere nearby, we were suddenly terrified.

The sound was so loud it felt like it was vibrating through every molecule in our bodies, and after we got over the initial shock, we both jumped in the Jeep.

Whatever it was, it was close and had undoubtedly been watching us, even though I hadn't felt any sense of foreboding. All I knew was that we needed to get out of there.

Except the Jeep wouldn't start.

I tried and tried to start it, but the battery seemed deader than a doorknob. I know batteries on their last legs will start just fine until they won't, giving up the ghost with no warning, but this battery wasn't that old. It actually seemed more like an electrical problem, like the starter wasn't getting any electrical current—just like Miles' car had acted, I realized.

Maggie had reached over and locked my door, and when I looked up, I could understand why. I think she was too shocked to say anything, and I admire her for even having the sensibility to lock the door, though I didn't think it was going to make much difference when I saw what she was looking at.

It seemed that three large men had come up from the creek below us, the same place where Miles' car had landed, but as they came closer and emerged from the bushes, I could see they weren't human. Not even close.

At that point, time seemed to become warped or something. I can't even begin to describe it, but it was kind of like being underwater. Maggie and I discussed it later, and she'd felt the same sensation.

Everything seemed to happen in slow motion, as if there was something in the atmosphere slowing these creatures down, like I said, as if they were underwater. It was the most bizarre thing I've ever experienced.

They came over to the Jeep, and I knew then and there what they were intending to do—they were going to push us over the side of the embankment, just like they'd done the car. These creatures had to be incredibly strong.

Up to then, they hadn't even looked inside, but as they were starting to push our Jeep sideways over the edge of the road, one of them stuck its face up to the window on Maggie's side. I'll never forget it—it was intelligent but incredibly menacing with big black deepset eyes and dark skin stretched taut across a face that was almost human.

And this is why I think Maggie being there saved my life, for it stopped pushing. We could hear it making sounds to its friends that were like some kind of language, and they stopped pushing, too. And with that, they left.

Why else would they have changed their minds if not for seeing Maggie? I don't understand it, but maybe they didn't want to harm a woman. Maggie has a very kind face, and maybe they recognized how sweet she was. Who knows?

And it was then that the Jeep started right up. I'll never figure that one out, though I have since read that others have had similar things happen with encounters.

But Rusty, have you noticed how I keep avoiding the word Bigfoot and use words like creature instead? After all these years, I still haven't come to grips with this.

I drove on back down the road, and it wasn't but a half mile before we saw someone who was kind of trying to half hide in the bushes along the road while still walking along. I stopped when I realized it was Miles, the fellow who owned the hounds. He seemed surprised to see me, but quickly got in, Maggie slipping into the back. She later told me she wanted to be behind him, not in front of him, as he looked half nuts.

He asked about his dogs, and I told him they were fine, and he could have them back anytime. He thanked us, but soon devolved into an incoherent mess—muttering and even crying. I think as soon as he knew his dogs were OK he just let it all hang out and kind of lost it.

In all honesty, he was kind of worrying me, as he seemed like he'd totally gone over the edge (no pun intended). I guessed he'd been in the car when it was pushed off the road, for he had some pretty good scratches on his face, though he didn't seem to have any serious injuries.

Maggie always has a level head, no matter what the situation, and she told me later she'd very quietly called the sheriff and asked them to have a deputy meet us at the bottom of the road, which they did. In fact, there were two deputies, and they took Miles to the hospital.

I felt like I should've gone to a hospital, too—a mental hospital. I've never felt so disoriented in my life, and after the adrenaline wore off, I went into what must've been a state of shock. I sat in my chair in the living room for hours, just staring at the wall. Maggie seemed to take it all better, though she went through some sleepless nights afterwards. Me, I was so exhausted from not being able to sleep that I later didn't have that problem.

We had the hounds for a couple more days, then Sheriff Jim called to tell me Miles' daughter had arrived and would be coming to get them, as Miles was just now getting out of the hospital.

She showed up shortly thereafter and seemed like a really nice caring person, maybe in her early 30's. The hounds seemed really happy to see her, so we handed them off without any worry.

We asked how her dad was doing, and she said she and her husband had come to take him home. They'd only been around him a few hours, but he seemed a little off to her, not as lively or something, but she felt he would gradually get better once he got back home.

She added that he seemed to have complete amnesia concerning what had happened, not even recalling going up there in the first place. She was worried about that, and probably rightly so, though maybe it would be for the best not to remember, for who knows what actually happened?

Maggie and I had our own problems to deal with from the experience, mostly in the form of nightmares, but as time went on, we both seemed to recover. I had a couple of more tows up in that area, though on different roads, but nothing like that, just straightforward get 'em out of the ditch kinds of things. And like I said, I never went alone.

Not long after, we decided to sell the house and leave. It wasn't long until we were on our way out to southern California, where her sister lived.

Several months later, I got a letter from Miles, forwarded from Ed. I was really surprised, but in it, he thanked me for taking care of his dogs, saying that if I hadn't taken them, they probably would've died. He said he'd gradually started to recall what had happened, and basically, he'd been in the car when it was pushed over the edge, but had miraculously been uninjured.

He'd seen what pushed it over and suspected the strange creatures would come back, so he'd managed to sneak away and had hidden in a nearby small cave for the rest of the night. Because he was somewhat underground, it was warmer and kept him from freezing.

Sure enough, he'd heard them looking for him, and they'd actually even come to the cave's entrance, but apparently hadn't seen him. He'd waited for daylight, and was getting ready to try to make a break when they came back. He felt like they would've come in, except they were too big.

He said he lay there in terror in that cave all day and through the next night, then gradually got up his courage, as he knew he would eventually die if he didn't get out. He made his way back to the road the following day. By then he was dehydrated and hungry and was losing contact with reality, such that it was.

Finally, he said he knew people would wonder why he'd been out there in the first place and had refused to go back with us. He'd come upon hard times, he said, having just lost his job as an airlines agent, and since someone told him there were jobs in Montana, he'd decided to leave Minnesota.

He didn't have enough money for a motel, so had driven out into the boonies to spend the night. But once out there, his hounds had heard something and started baying, which terrified him.

He'd tried to drive out but his car wouldn't start, and so he'd called for help. Once I'd actually arrived and couldn't start his car, he said he kind of panicked, knowing he didn't have the money for a motel or car repair and decided to camp there, glad I took his dogs.

He said not going out with me was a decision he deeply regretted, as it had changed his entire life, and he now had difficulty being alone. He was living with his daughter and had finally gotten a good job, but the entire event had taken its toll. I found a one-hundred dollar bill in the envelope.

I was glad to hear from him, and I gave the money to Maggie, who donated it to the local animal shelter. I actually wanted nothing to do with it, as I knew that whatever we might buy would always make me think of him, which would in turn make me think of something I'd just as soon forget.

And there wasn't enough money on Earth to make me want to remember what I saw out there. In fact, I'd give almost everything I own to be able to forget it.

4

HEART OF DARKNESS

I was contacted by a friend, a fellow fishing guide, who said he'd met a guy who had an interesting story he'd like to share with me next time I was in Montana.

I know the microbrewery this guy works for, and next time I was in his neighborhood, I stopped in for a beer and a pretty good tale.

Is it true? I don't know, but Andy told it with such conviction that if it wasn't true, he should become an actor. I do know the campground he speaks of pretty well, and it is definitely right smack in the middle of perfect Bigfoot habitat. —Rusty

My name's Andy, and thanks in advance for giving me the chance to tell this story to someone who will listen without being judgmental. I'm really tired of being told, whether outright or by body language, that I'm nuts.

When I was in school, we read a book called *Heart of Darkness*. I don't recall anything about it except that I think it was set in Africa, and I'm not even sure about that. But I do know it had a good title, and after all this happened, I felt like it described exactly where I'd been.

It all started when I got a job as a host in a campground in the mountains about 30 miles north of the little town of Gardiner, Montana, which is just north of Yellowstone National Park. I remember the job description well, because it said you had to be self-sufficient, as there was no cell service and you didn't have any backup unless you drove down lower to where you could call out.

I remember this because it almost made me decide not to take the job, though the word job is kind of misleading, since it was a volunteer position with the Forest Service.

It wasn't a large campground, and the description on the Internet said it was mostly visited by people who liked to hike, though there was some fishing and a nearby petrified forest of trees that had died in one of the volcanic explosions from the nearby Absaroka Mountains. There wasn't much else—except grizzly bears.

Anyway, as an aside, after this happened a few years ago, I went on a Bigfoot binge. I read everything I could get my hands on—books and forums and blogs on the Internet—everything. I totally immersed myself in Bigfoot stuff for a year, and I have to say that I haven't read one encounter that was anything like mine.

This actually makes me glad, because I wouldn't wish it on anyone. Fortunately for me I'm a laid-back guy who isn't easily rattled, or I would be a nut cake, though some of my friends think I am anyway. I finally quit telling my story to just anyone.

Well, in spite of my reservations, I went ahead and applied for the job. I don't think there was a lot of competition, if any, because I got it, to my surprise. I guess I was as qualified as anyone, which isn't saying much, as it doesn't take a lot to hang around a campground, clean a few fire pits, and make sure everything's going OK.

The main thing is being self-sufficient and knowing how to deal with people, and I'm pretty good at both, though my normal way of dealing with people is usually to just leave them be. Of course, you can't always do that when you're running a campground.

Why was I so worried about not having cell communication? Well, it mostly had to do with the fact that the campground is part of the Greater Yellowstone Ecosystem and crawling with grizzlies. It's actually right on the park boundary.

I didn't worry about myself, as growing up in Montana, I've found most bears will leave you alone, but I was worried about some of the crazies that I might have to deal with, as I knew the campground was often filled with people wanting to see bears.

There was a big ranch on the way up there that had dude accommodations, and part of the attraction was the grizzlies that would come into the ranch meadows to dig grubs and eat grasses. People would stay there just for that reason, as well as drive up to hang out by the pastures to take photos. In fact, you were more likely to see bears in this area than you were in Yellowstone, so it got to where a lot of people went up there, and still do.

For some reason, I got the idea that the place might turn into a Night of the Grizzlies scenario and I'd be responsible, all on my lonesome. Ironically, few bears came around that summer, and the reason why is part of this story.

I'm from Big Timber, which isn't all that far from the campground, just a couple of hours. One reason I chose this place was so I wouldn't be too far from home, though I no longer actually had a house there, but I did have family.

I'd gone to Montana State in Bozeman, getting a degree in Economics, then had worked as the Economic Development Director for the City of Bozeman. My main job was to encourage businesses to move there and thereby provide more and better jobs.

Ironically, I myself was left unemployed after working there a number of years, as I didn't get along with the new City Manager. She put a black mark on my job history that basically ruined my employment opportunities. She was later herself fired, but it was too late to help me.

I mention all this because it resulted in my losing my house and everything I owned, which is why I ended up living in a campground. Not only that, it meant I had no place to go, and this meant I stayed there long after I probably should've left.

To get to the campground, you cross the Yellowstone River, where the countryside is just scrub sagebrush and juniper trees, dry and rocky with nary a hint of what's to come. But as you climb, you're soon in lush meadows with ranches, and then you gradually get into forest and high mountains. The campground is in a heavily wooded valley of pines and aspen along a creek in some of the wildest country in Montana, the Gallatin Mountains. I found out later that there have been a number of Bigfoot sightings there.

It was early June, and there were still snowbanks under some of the trees and a chill in the air. I was actually pretty pleased when I first got there, as it was so quiet and pretty, the forest ranger showing me my site and setting up a campground host sign as I backed my little Chalet trailer into my spot.

We then sat at a picnic table after he'd showed me around and told me my duties. I was there mostly to keep the campground clean and provide a presence, keeping people from burning the forest down or cutting down trees for wood, that kind of thing. A ranger would come up every so often to check on things, and I could come out for two days a week to resupply and whatnot, though I had to be there on weekends.

I really liked this ranger guy, Tim, and as we sat there drinking coffee from his Thermos, he mentioned that the previous camp host had been there every season for the past nine years, but after a couple of encounters with a grizzly, he'd been frightened and decided to move on.

Tim then told me they'd hazed this particular bear off with bear bangers, which are kind of like firecrackers, and he was going to leave me with some, as well as an extra couple of cans of bear spray. He said I should be very careful to warn campers not to hike without spray. A few years back, a local hunter had actually been killed by a griz in that area, though they thought it was a different bear. If a bear started hanging around the campground, they would try to trap and relocate it.

Well, Tim finally left, I popped up my trailer, a hard-side A-frame, got things organized, then made some sandwiches and kicked back in my anti-gravity chair, a fancy name for a foldable recliner. I immediately noticed how totally quiet it was up there.

Tim had said that on quiet days, I might see any number of animals, since I was basically in Yellowstone, including black bear, elk, moose, wolves, foxes, eagles, bighorn sheep, mountain goats, and yes, the griz. I should always carry my bear spray, even when outside just sitting at my picnic table.

I was in paradise. The valley below me, where the Yellowstone River ran, was actually called Paradise Valley, but I felt it didn't hold a candle to where I was, as it had too many people.

I'd discovered the real deal, and I can say that my first day there was one I cherish in my heart, and I wish it had stayed that way. When I think of the perfect place and the perfect life, I think of that day.

Have you ever done something exhausting, like maybe drive straight through to some place far away or taken a long tiring hike, maybe farther than you'd intended? Remember what it's like to be able to kick back, safe and secure, knowing your troubles are over for at least the time being?

That's how I felt, like I'd found a refuge from the storm of my life, and I had a great sense of relief. It's like you focus on your surroundings and how nice everything is instead of what you need to do and all your problems.

But unbeknownst to me, I would soon come to realize it was temporary. Instead of paradise, I'd been thrust into the heart of darkness.

I spent the rest of the day walking around the campground, checking out the creek, and just getting familiar with my surroundings. It wasn't long until the sun began to set and it got chilly, so I went inside and turned on my little propane heater and settled in.

I had brought a number of books, and I started reading one about a fellow named Buzz Holmstrom who built his own boat and floated the Green River down in Utah way before anyone else was doing it. He was an independent and capable guy, and the more I read, the more I admired his determination. I wanted to be more like that, especially since my career plans had gone south. Maybe I'd move down there and become a boatman, a raft guide.

After an hour or so, since I didn't want to use up my headlamp batteries, I put the book away, put on my down coat, and stepped outside.

I was stunned by the night sky. Even though most of it was blocked by the trees, I could see part of the Milky Way blazing in a giant arc. It glowed like the lights from a big city, millions of bright dots all melting together. I knew each was a star, and it took my breath away.

I wanted to get out of the trees and see more of the sky, so I worked my way along the campground road a ways, trying to find more of a clearing. I hadn't brought my headlamp, as I'd intended to simply step out for a minute, nor had I left any of my trailer lights on in an effort to save my battery, as I had solar, and I knew it wouldn't recharge very quickly in the trees. Besides, I wanted to see the night sky without any light pollution.

And see the night sky I did. I didn't realize it at the time, but it would be one of the few times I felt comfortable being out in the dark like that.

I was sitting on a picnic table a couple of sites down from mine, stargazing, when I finally started to feel a sense of uneasiness. I'd felt this before out in the dark alone, and I figured it was just my survival instincts kicking in.

On top of that, seeing the immensity of the curtain of stars above me was beginning to make me feel insignificant. I knew this could lead to depression, as I already felt pretty insignificant anyway, given the state of my life, so I decided to go back inside.

But as I walked back to where my little white trailer should've been, I found only darkness. I'd somehow missed it, even though I knew I was going in the right direction. There was enough starlight that it should be visible in the dark, but I saw nothing, though I'd only been two sites down and had followed the road.

I stopped, recalling a time I'd done this with a tent. I'd been volunteering with a group helping build a boardwalk across a wetlands, and I'd pitched my tent quite a ways away from the rest in order to not be kept up, as I knew there would be partying well into the night.

After sitting around a big campfire with everyone for awhile, I'd headed for my tent, but I couldn't find it. It was a potentially serious situation, as we were on the edge of wilderness, and I could get myself really lost.

I'd stopped and waited until my night vision got better, which will typically take a good 30 minutes after you've been around light, whether it be a flashlight beam or a campfire. I finally was able to see well enough that when I backtracked I found the tent. Sure enough, I'd walked right past it.

So, I decided to go back to the picnic table and wait until my night vision kicked in, even though I was feeling pretty uneasy. My first night there, and I'd broken all the rules—I was out with no bear spray, no flashlight, and no common sense. I felt like an idiot.

I admit it was pretty spooky sitting out at that picnic table in the dark, thinking of bears, the awe of the night sky now replaced by nervousness. But finally, like before, my night vision gradually acclimated, and I was able to quickly find my trailer, its white fiberglass skin a mere shadow in the starlight.

I was never so happy to go inside and close the door. I've since wondered if there wasn't more to my getting disoriented than I'd thought.

In spite of my stupid little escapade, I slept like a baby and woke refreshed early the next morning. That next day was again spent in paradise, as no one showed up and I had the place all to myself. I was as happy as I'd ever been in my life.

This went on for several days, as it was early enough in the season that there wasn't anyone around. After a few days there, I decided to hike to the Gallatin Petrified Forest. It was pretty famous, an entire forest of trees buried in an upright position when debris flows from a volcanic eruption killed them.

Frozen in time, the 50-million-year-old trees stood exactly as they had eons ago. They weren't killed by the Yellowstone volcano, but rather by eruptions from the nearby Absaroka Mountains.

The trail was well-marked, starting just past the campground, and I'd read a little about it before coming. It climbed 750 feet in a half-mile, switchbacking and ending in the debris flows, where the trees stood. It sounded like a nice way to spend a few hours while also getting some exercise.

I packed a lunch, putting it in my daypack with some water and a jacket. I hooked my bear spray onto my belt, then headed out. It was a beautiful day, and I was excited to see the trees.

I'd gone a short distance up the trail when I stopped to catch my breath, and as I stood there, I thought I saw movement ahead. I could tell it was dark brown, and I was hoping it was a deer and not a bear. I kind of stepped off the trail to the side, hoping whatever it was wouldn't see me.

I could soon see that it was indeed a bear, and a rather big one at that. It was ambling along the trail, coming my way, and I wasn't sure whether I should backtrack and hope to stay ahead of it or stand my ground and hope it would leave when it saw me. I took out my bear spray and undid the safety.

It was now on the trail a mere 50 feet or so ahead of me, and I could easily see it was a big boar grizzly, and I do mean a big one. It quickly spotted me and stopped, ears forward, alert, absolute in its role of king of the forest. I was almost shaking by then, wondering how a can of spray could possibly stop an animal so large.

It now looked like it was going to charge, the nape of its neck standing up and its eyes staring directly into mine. I knew I shouldn't be staring back, as it would perceive that as aggression, but I couldn't help myself.

I nervously held the can of bear spray up, half afraid to move, hoping it would see it and run away. Looking back, it seems silly now to think a bear would have a clue what bear spray was, but I thought maybe it had been sprayed before.

And just as I knew it was going to charge, it suddenly turned its head to its left, raised its nose as if smelling something, then immediately turned in the opposite direction and literally hurtled itself off the trail and through the thick trees, crashing along as fast as it could.

Something had scared it, but what would scare a big boar grizzly? It was obviously a male from its size, and grizzly males are pretty much afraid of nothing. Females and cubs are afraid of the males, as they'll kill the cubs, but nothing scares a big male griz—or so I thought until then.

I was so totally unhinged by this that I turned and quickly made my way back to camp, basically hiding in my trailer, bear spray ready.

Was this the same bear that had terrorized the other camp host, making him leave? Tim hadn't told me any of the details, but he had said the bear hadn't been trapped, which meant it could easily come back. And what had scared it?

I couldn't answer these questions, so I just stayed inside the trailer and read my book, trying to forget my fears, then I finally went back outside when I realized some campers had shown up.

I was very relieved to see them, several cars of hikers from Billings. I even helped them set up their tents, and they reciprocated by inviting me to a fajita dinner. I left as soon as it got dark, warning them to keep their food in the nearby bear boxes.

The next day, the hikers took off on the eight-mile trail to nearby Ramshorn Peak, a 10,000+ foot summit along the Gallatin Crest where you can see many of the region's ranges, some which were in Yellowstone, like the Sphinx, Mount Cowen, and Electric Peak. I hadn't been up that trail, but had read about it and was hoping to hike it before I left in the fall.

I spent the day just hanging around, and again had dinner with the hikers. That night, we were all treated to the howls of the wolf pack that lives in the area, which were both thrilling and just a little scary. I hadn't considered that maybe it was wolves that had scared the bear, but I now figured that had to have been it.

The hikers went on another hike the next day, but came back early and went home, as the weekend was over. Even though I'd been cherishing my solitude, I was sad to see them go. I knew it was because I had that big bear in the back of my mind and now felt insecure.

Let me describe my little Chalet trailer so you have a feel for what I had in terms of security.

You've probably seen these little fold-up A-frame trailers—there's another brand called an A-Liner. They basically fold down when you're towing, but then you pop up the roof and two sides when camping.

They're not canvas, like most other folding trailers, but have a lightweight fiberglass skin on aluminum. So, you basically have a roof over you that's made of two sections plus two smaller side sections, and what holds them together are some clips on the inside of the trailer. They're not real solid, like a non-folding trailer would be, and can be downright dangerous in high winds, as the sides can collapse if you don't use special cables.

They're more secure than a canvas tent trailer, but not as secure as a regular one, though the parks will let you use them in places where there are bears and where canvas trailers aren't allowed, like at Fishing Bridge in Yellowstone. I loved mine, as it was not only easy to pull, but the A-shaped roof made it feel really roomy inside with its high peaked roof.

Well, my newfound buddies were gone, and I missed the security of having others around, even though I knew it wouldn't be long before things warmed up and the campground would be full most of the time. I knew I'd be wishing for my solitude. I started thinking about how isolated I was, especially with no phone.

That night seemed extraordinarily quiet, though I thought it was probably because the previous two nights had been busier. But it almost seemed unnatural, like the normal night sounds were missing. I tried to figure out what a normal night sound was up there in the timber, and I decided it was the call of the owl and the occasional snorts of nearby deer.

There was nothing but a deep silence, and it turned out to be the night of my first unsettling dream. There really wasn't much to it plot wise, but dark emotions and a feeling of dread were its main components. It took awhile for me to realize it was a dream and not real.

What happened in the dream was I woke up hearing something trying to get inside the trailer. It was making a quiet scratching noise at the door, as if trying not to wake me. I quietly got up and grabbed my bear spray and very carefully pulled up one corner of the curtain to look outside.

Whatever it was had apparently heard me, for it turned and walked away, but I could make out the shape of a really large creature's back, and it seemed to be walking on two legs. I know bears can do this, but it seemed even larger than the boar griz I'd seen.

Like I said, it took me awhile after I'd woken up to realize it had been a dream. My bear spray was right where I'd left it the night before. It was still dark outside, and I was half-afraid to look out, but I finally pulled the curtain aside enough to see out. I could see nothing but darkness.

It was five a.m., and I knew there was no way I was going to get back to sleep, so I got up and made some coffee, using my headlamp, for some reason half afraid to turn on the lights and let anyone know I was awake.

As I sat there drinking coffee in the dark, I listened carefully for anything unusual outside. It was then that I heard the wolf pack, but they seemed far away. It was all pretty eerie.

It was Monday, and since I hadn't been anywhere since coming to the campground two weeks before, I decided I'd go into town and get some fresh fruit and greens, walk around in civilization for a bit, and try to clear my head. I had the urge to just hook up my trailer and head back to Big Timber, and I really wish I had done that.

Instead, I drove to Livingston, which is the opposite direction of Gardiner and a lot bigger. I resupplied at the grocery store, hung out at Sacajawea Park for a bit watching the geese, then found myself at the local sporting goods store.

Before I was done, I'd purchased a Remington 700 rifle and plenty of ammo, as well as a pair of night-vision goggles. Was I being paranoid? No doubt, and some may question if it's a good idea for paranoid people to be armed, but there I was.

This about did in my meager savings, and in retrospect, I would've been better off using the money to rent a space in a small RV park there and gone to work at minimum wage somewhere.

It's amazing what fear can do to one. Instead of leaving the campground, I felt some misplaced sense of loyalty to Tim and the Forest Service to stay until autumn like I'd said I would.

I realized later that this loyalty was really a one-way street, for none of them would've thought much about it if I'd left, given that it was a volunteer position and was turning into a less than optimal experience. I think most people would've left right then and there.

But it was just a dream, I told myself. I had let my imagination get the best of me, and that was no reason to give up on what had been a pretty good thing so far. But I really didn't want to go back to the campground, and seeing how I had an extra sleeping bag in my pickup, I went out to a big field not far from town and spent the night there. I could see houses in the distance, and it felt good.

I had breakfast in town the next day, then messed around down by the Yellowstone River talking to a couple of fishermen, taking my time getting back to the campground.

When I finally got back, I felt better, having gained the perspective one gets from getting away for awhile—as well as now being armed, even though I hadn't shot a rifle since my dad took me to the shooting range when I was in high school. Even then, I'd been a terrible shot.

There was no one in the campground, and I again felt a sense of uneasiness, hoping someone would show up. As with most campgrounds, people tended to come more towards the weekends. It was late afternoon when I got back, so I basically just spent the evening reading and went to bed early. It was a quiet night.

The next day, Tim, the forest ranger, showed up around noon to check on things, and I was glad to see him. I made some coffee, then we sat at the picnic table and talked, just as we'd done when I first arrived.

I told him about the big boar grizzly, and he expressed concern. I told him I'd just bought a rifle, but he didn't react at all like I thought he would, but told me to be extra cautious with it. He didn't think it would even slow down a big bear, plus if I were to actually shoot and kill one, I'd be in a courtroom explaining why, even if it had been in self-defense, as it was an endangered species.

He encouraged me to stick with the bear spray, then explained that most bears will bluff charge anyway, and I shouldn't be shooting at them, as bear spray was best. The more we talked, the more I got the feeling that he wasn't being totally honest with me about the previous camp host, and there was more to the story.

Well, after Tim told me the rifle probably wouldn't even slow down a bear, it left me feeling a little resentful at the sales clerk in the sporting goods store who'd told me the rifle was perfect for shooting bears. He hadn't bothered to educate me on anything, which I knew wasn't his job, but he'd obviously just wanted to make the sale. I decided to return the rifle the next time I went to town. I didn't want to shoot a bear anyway, I was just scared of them.

Well, talk to anyone who's served as a camp host for very long and they'll have plenty of stories to tell about strange people, and that night was my turn to experience the weirdness that humans can exhibit.

It was dark when several carloads of people showed up, basically spreading out in all seven sites and taking over the campground. They had tents and were within the rules and regulations as to the number of people per site, so I just went with the flow, though I had a feeling these were not your typical campers. I don't know what sites there cost these days, but it was $7 a site then, so it's not like they had to shell out a lot of money, which was maybe why they'd picked the place, as they looked pretty rag-tag.

To this day I have no idea who they were or what they were doing, but it seemed to reverberate through the forest, waking something that came to visit after they were gone, or at least that's how it seemed.

I was sitting in my trailer, checking out my new Bushnell night-vision goggles, looking out the window into the darkness, amazed at how much I could see. Even though it was dark, I could easily make out trees, picnic tables, and the new campers, who seemed to be milling around a big campfire.

As I watched, they put on strange-looking masks, and someone started drumming. They all danced around the fire, chanting. Like I said, I have no idea what they were doing, but it was weird.

This went on and on, and I remember noting that it was late and they were making a lot of noise way beyond quiet time. But since I wasn't even tired and there was no one else in the campground, I decided to let them be. Actually, I was having fun watching them and playing around with my new toy.

They finally quieted down around midnight, though I could still see them sitting around. Oddly enough, they were all gone when I got up at dawn. Since I'd been up really late, I didn't even want to get up, but I'd had another unsettling dream and couldn't sleep.

This time, I'd dreamt that whatever had been trying to get inside my trailer had managed to open the door and come inside. I couldn't make anything out for sure in the dark—it was just a large black shadow. It stood above me, and I could see its head almost touched the peak of the A-frame ceiling, which was several feet above my head, and I'm almost six-feet tall.

I remember in the dream wishing I had my night-vision goggles so I could see it better, but then the thought came into my mind that I was better off not knowing. I was terrified, so I closed my eyes, not wanting it to know I was awake.

After some time, it left, again leaving me with a feeling of despair and wanting to flee. I vowed to leave as soon as it got light. To heck with promising to stay until fall.

After it was light, I examined the lock on the door. I decided it had to have been a dream, as nothing was broken. I then again sat at the picnic table, drinking coffee and trying to decide if I should leave, even though I'd earlier vowed I would and had even packed up a few things.

But where would I go? Part of my plan was to stay here until the end of summer, when I could head east and stay at a friend's place in Oklahoma, as she was going to have knee surgery and wanted me around to help out. If I left, I'd just be looking for other places to camp until then.

Before long, more campers started arriving, and I decided that since I now had company, I'd stay, taking each day at a time.

As I sat at the picnic table, I tried to sort out why I was having these weird dreams. I'd once read that the brain tries to solve problems when dreaming. Were the dark shadow forms somehow representative of something I needed to complete, some problem plaguing me that I hadn't properly addressed?

It seemed possible, since I was living such an unsettled life in terms of my future. I'd also read that most dreaming happens during REM sleep, when the emotional centers of the brain are more active and the logical parts are inhibited. So it would make sense that dreams would be emotionally charged and not logical.

Thinking about all this made me feel better, and I resolved to do some serious contemplation about my future. I needed to do more than just float around from place to place. All this thinking left me feeling better, like if I solved these problems the dreams would go away.

But that night, even though there were other campers around and I'd tried to meditate awhile on solving my problems, I had another weird dream.

This was similar to the previous one where a dark form came inside my trailer, but this time it actually bent down over me. I could feel its hot fetid breath in my face, and it was all I could do to not yell out.

I could make out its large eyes, which seemed like endless dark pools that I could fall into if I weren't careful, and it seemed like it was calling out to me, telling me to follow, though I had no idea where it would take me, and I actually heard nothing, as if it was all in my mind.

Unlike the previous dream when I'd feigned being asleep, I couldn't close my eyes and stared at it against my will. It had an almost magnetic presence, and I was actually thinking about getting up and getting dressed so I could follow it. It suddenly turned and left, and I couldn't tell if it even went through the door or not.

I woke and had the presence to jump up and look out the windows with my night-vision goggles, but I saw nothing. Once again, the door was still locked, and I knew it had to have been another dream, even though it felt real. I had an incredible adrenaline rush and realized I was sweating, even though the nights up there were chilly.

I got up at dawn and left, going down into the town of Gardiner. I spent most of the day there, just hanging around, standing on the bridge over the Yellowstone River watching rafters go by, then wandering through various shops in town, which was funny, as I normally hate shopping.

But it all felt very comforting. I decided to go back and gather up my stuff and get out, so around mid-afternoon, I headed back up the hill to the campground.

But once there, it seemed different, like the idyllic place I'd felt when I first arrived. There were campers around, and I visited some, then decided to spend just one more night. I felt guilty for leaving, my misplaced sense of duty again rearing its head.

I was again invited to dinner and campfire talk with some climbers from Idaho, and I had a great time, wondering why I would even consider leaving over stupid dreams that weren't even real. Climbers are generally can-do kind of people, and they left me feeling a sense of determination and optimism, like I could conquer the dreams and get on with my life, though I certainly didn't mention anything to them.

I slept like a baby for the next few nights. It was almost as if the dreams knew they now couldn't get to me. But fast forward to another Monday when the campground was empty, and things took a turn for the worse.

It had been a quiet day with no one around, and I'd enjoyed the peace and solitude, actually writing some in a journal I'd started in an attempt to help me sort out my future direction. I'd decided to go up to Livingston the next day and get on the Internet there at one of the espresso cafes and see if I could get a real job. In all honesty, I'd kind of quit looking some time before, having gotten discouraged.

But, like they say, it was not to be. That night, I was sitting outside at my picnic table, my night-vision goggles at hand, enjoying the night sky again for the first time in ages, when I heard the howling.

I at first thought it was the wolf pack, as it was far enough away to not be very distinct. But as I listened, I was suddenly shocked to hear a reply that sounded like it was coming from up the trail to the petrified trees, and it was no wolf.

We've all heard the description "blood curdling," but until then, I had no idea what that really meant. That sound actually made me feel like my blood had stopped flowing through my veins. It was so loud it gave me an instant headache, and I felt disoriented, whereas moments before, all had been normal.

I can only describe it as a high-pitched scream that at first sounded like a mountain lion but disintegrated into a deep throaty bellow, then a low growl. It was the most menacing sound I'd ever heard, and I knew it was close.

Even though I now felt somewhat groggy and sluggish, I managed to get inside my trailer and lock the door. Once inside, I felt better, and I got out my rifle and loaded it. I knew it would be a sleepless night, so I made myself some instant coffee and settled in to see what would happen. I was suddenly feeling very competent and determined, even though scared. I was tired of being afraid, and I was going to put an end to all this.

In retrospect, my attitude was one of total denial. There was no way I could win a battle with whatever it was, as it had to be very large and fearless. I recalled what Tim had said about a rifle not being adequate to shoot a big griz, but I was willing to go down shooting. I laid the loaded rifle on the foot of my bed where it would be handy.

Now, up to then, I'd thought I'd been dreaming, but when I heard the distant howls come closer, followed by the nearby scream, I knew there was something out there way beyond my ken.

I'd heard of Bigfoot, but I wasn't prepared to accept it as something real. And like I said, I read every Bigfoot account on the Internet after all this, and all I can say is that seeing one is a life-altering event. Sure, it's scary as heck, but it also challenges your concept of reality.

And see one I did—not just one, but several, for the screams kept getting closer and closer, and as I held my goggles to the window, I realized they were out there, and they weren't just passing through. My goggles weren't the best, and all I could make out were dark shadows, but that was all it took to leave me quaking in my boots.

And then the strangest feeling came over me, a feeling that I belonged with them and should go out and meet them. They were benign, in spite of their terrifying calls, and they meant me no harm. I felt that same magnetic pull, and I went over to unlock the door.

Just then, my rifle went off.

I swear I was nowhere near it, but it just shot, just as if I'd been there and pulled the trigger. I still have that little Chalet trailer, and the bullet hole is plain as day on the inside, though I've caulked over it on the outside to keep the weather out.

Now, I can say that really freaked me out, because as soon as the rifle went off, I heard a scream right next to the trailer. I'll never know if the bullet hit one of them, but it did scare them off, for I immediately knew they were gone. I could no longer see anything through my goggles, and the feeling of magnetism was gone, replaced again by a determination that they weren't going to get to me.

I sat there all night, waiting for them to come back, rifle nearby, but it was as quiet as could be, no owls, no deer, no wolves, nothing, though I could sometimes hear my own heart beating.

The next day the campground was full again, and I again decided to stay. By then, my stint as a host was more than half over, and I knew I could make it through until fall. For some reason, I was no longer afraid.

A couple of days later, the campground was empty again, and I'd been busy cleaning fire pits and raking sites. I'd left my trailer locked, but when I went back for lunch, I found my rifle gone. The lock wasn't broken—it was if someone had picked it, which made me think back to all my dreams.

I wondered if maybe they hadn't been dreams at all—and that thought gave me the creeps.

Had these creatures picked my lock? Remember how I said that I haven't read one encounter that was anything like mine? Well, this is why. I think Bigfoot knows how to use tools, and why not? They have hands just like we do, with opposable thumbs.

I also think they stole my rifle, because a couple of days later, I heard a distant shot, and I suspected it was my Remington.

I think they took it, and it accidentally fired again, as the sound came from an area that's thick timber with no trails. Let me tell you why I think this.

Months later, I stumbled on a news article that talked about the Remington 700, saying that thousands of Remington 700 customers complained that the trigger mechanism could fire without the trigger being squeezed, and a lot of lawsuits had been filed alleging injury or death because of this. There was even an investigative TV series about it saying that over two dozen deaths and hundreds of injuries had been attributed to inadvertent discharges of the rifles.

I know that's what happened in my trailer, and I suspect it happened again when I heard the gunshot in the distance. I've since wondered what might transpire if an angry Bigfoot knew how to use a rifle, but hopefully it scared them and is now lying forgotten somewhere in the timber in the Montana backcountry.

The rest of my time at the campground was uneventful, maybe because the campground was pretty much full all the time, but I also think it was because I'd scared the Bigfoot away. When you think about it, our ability to develop and use firearms has probably been the most effective means we've had for survival out in the backwoods where predators would just as soon eat us.

I'm not saying Bigfoot is like that, but if nothing else, they have the ability to literally scare us to death. I've never been so frightened in my life, bar none.

After I finished out my stay at the campground, I felt a new sense of strength, and I went back to Big Timber for a week or two, then to Oklahoma, where I helped out my friend.

I then went back to Montana, where I went to work in a micro-brewery. After awhile, I ended up becoming their marketing manager, since I was good at it.

I really like my job, though I'm not getting rich, but I get to live in Montana. I still like to camp, except I won't go alone any more, which is probably a good thing, and even though I've been back to that particular campground again for the day, I really have no desire to camp there.

I'm happy to sit on my deck at home and look out over the mountains, thinking of what's really out there, somehow glad it's still a wild enough place that Bigfoot can survive, but too wild for me—and at times, way too dark.

5

THE EXPERIMENT

As you may know, my wife Sarah is a geologist, and sometimes she meets some really interesting people in the course of her job. She met Hank, a fellow geologist, at a conference, and this led to her meeting Hank's wife, Vickie.

Sarah and Vickie got to talking, and when Vickie told my wife about her encounter, Sarah asked her to contact me. Vickie told me the following story over the phone, and I recorded it with her permission, though she asked me to change the place and her name, which I did. This is one of the more interesting Bigfoot stories I've ever heard. —Rusty

Rusty, as you know, I told some of this to your wife, but there's really a lot more than I had time to tell her over lunch. Since you've agreed to change the details enough that people can't guess who I am, here goes. I hope you find it as interesting as I did while actually experiencing it.

As Sarah probably told you, at the time I was a postgrad researcher at a Montana university. I'm a physical anthropologist, and my specialty is genetics and behavior—not just genetics in general, but epigenetics, which is a very complex subject, involving a detailed knowledge of biology and how DNA works.

I'll try not to get into too much depth, but basically, epigenetics refers to changes that affect gene expression, which can be environmental. These changes cause the DNA to be active or inactive, a trigger that turns things on and off and alters how genes are expressed without changing the underlying DNA sequence. Sometimes such changes can be inherited.

It gets complicated really fast, so bear with me. There's a lot of research being done in this area and it's becoming a hot topic, though I'm no longer active in researching it.

Let me give you an example of epigenetics. Let's say you have a set of identical twins, which means their DNA is also identical, and yet one is tall with freckles, and the other is normal height with no freckles. How can this be, since their genes are exactly the same?

Well, the one who's tall has a different diet from the other, maybe getting better nutrition, which triggers the gene for height, and he also spends more time in the sun, which turns on the gene for freckles. This is what epigenetics is about, environmental factors activating genes that are turned off. This is done through a molecule attaching itself to that DNA, and like I said, sometimes having that gene turned on is inheritable. So, the twin with freckles may have a kid who also has freckles but has never spent much time out in the sun. This is kind of an oversimplified example, but hopefully, you get the idea.

OK, so let's get back to Bigfoot, which your wife says you're interested in. How would this have anything at all to do with that topic?

Well, I've often wondered why babies at a very young age will exhibit fears of things they've never encountered, things their parents have never mentioned to them—I mean we're talking about five- or six-month olds who can't even talk yet.

If you show a baby a photo of a snake or spider, it will exhibit fear. Where did they get that? Some are afraid of snakes, and some of spiders, but usually not both. And the same holds for animals who are naturally afraid of predators, yet may have never been around them, like zoo animals. There's been a lot of research done in this area, and my specialty as a postdoctoral fellow was to combine this behavior with the study of epigenetics.

I believe that we can inherit information that's been part of our survival since the dawn of humankind, things like a fear of snakes. There are a lot of researchers who agree with me, and it's not my original idea. And you can probably see where I'm going with this in regards to Bigfoot and big hairy monsters in general, fear of which is found in most cultures. In other words, almost every culture has legends about big hairy monsters in some form or other.

So, if what we're seeing is an epigenetic memory, carried as a marker on our genes across many people around the world, what caused it? Were there really big hairy monsters around who threatened the human populations and migrated around the world?

I believe these monsters were real, and the finding of Gigantopithecus was a big plus in the support of that theory. Keep in mind that some researchers don't believe things like this are inheritable, but research has shown that when a parent experiences real trauma, the effects can be inherited by their babies, even if the trauma was long before the baby was even conceived, and we're also finding that these effects can be inherited from grandparents and maybe even farther back.

Now let's look at the Bigfoot mythology. When I started my research, I personally believed that Bigfoot was just a manifestation of the fear that we carried epigenetically about big hairy monsters. I had no belief or expectations for Bigfoot to still actually exist, I simply thought it was a remnant fear from people long ago living with things like Gigantopithecus, which was a huge primate, weighing up to 1300 pounds and standing over ten-feet tall, with an arm span of almost 12 feet.

Gigantopithecus would certainly give me nightmares, even though it was a vegetarian. Dating methods show that it was co-existent with early humans (Homo erectus) and existed for a million years, going extinct about 100,000 years ago, which would also mean it coexisted with Homo sapiens for tens of thousands of years.

Keep in mind that people also have inborn fears about predators in general, and we somehow naturally fear bears, mountain lions, etc. But there's something much more primal about our monster fears, and I personally believe the monsters were more like us in that they were cunning and could sometimes outsmart us, which other predators can't do. In other words, these creatures viewed us prey, whereas a bear views us more as something to kill if we get in its way, and even then, most predators will go out of their way to avoid humans. And bears don't typically come to your house at night and watch you through the windows.

Did Giganto hunt us? Did it kill our children? We think Giganto was a plant eater and not a carnivore, so it would actually have no reason to hunt humans, but perhaps there were others out there like it that did.

Were they intelligent adversaries, something to fear that could easily overcome us and eat us? Is it part of the reason we humans have developed into group animals for our protection, and why many of us are afraid to be alone out in the woods, even in the daytime? And why does this fear continue to haunt us, generation after generation, now that these monsters are long extinct? Why does this fear seem to be so deep in the human psyche?

These were all questions I wanted badly to answer, and my postdoc research was partially designed to do this, though I had to tread very carefully, as many of my colleagues were extremely skeptical about this entire subject.

Keep in mind that there was a big difference between Bigfoot researchers and me—they believed Bigfoot exists, and I didn't. I was merely looking for reasons for these fears that seem to be pretty much global among humans. I was an anthropologist looking for answers to a certain human behavior. I thought I was looking into the past, but I found I wasn't.

So how would one go about trying to determine what this was all about? Designing an experiment was extremely difficult, but I decided to go ahead and try, and the rest of this story deals with what behavioralists call a preliminary experiment, something designed to see if you're even on the right track before you get too invested in it.

Working in a university setting gave me all the experimental subjects I could ask for in the form of students. I wanted to see how people acted when they thought they were being threatened by something they didn't understand.

I needed to find a place that was remote and yet not so far from the university that the students would have trouble getting there. After doing some searching, I found a small fishing resort in northern Montana, only a couple of hours away.

I contacted the resort, and since it was late in the fall, they gave me a really good price. I rented the entire place for one night and the following day. It consisted of several cabins plus a small main lodge, which had a cafeteria and a big common room with a fireplace. My next step was to find some willing subjects and a couple of friends to help me conduct the experiment.

Sometimes we have enough in the budget to actually pay people who will be the subjects of our experiments, but pretty much all my budget had gone to renting the cabins, and I was worried that I wouldn't be able to get anyone to come out there.

But I shouldn't have worried, as I was inundated with kids wanting to get away for a night, especially for free. The kids could drive their own cars or carpool.

Of course, the kids had no idea what they were in for, as we'd advertised it in the school paper as a sociological experiment. Keep in mind that this was some time ago, and I'm not sure we could engage in something like this now, even if we had everyone sign a release form. Schools are much more likely to be sued these days, so are much more restrictive.

I'd cut it off at 12 kids. I wanted to put six in the two-bedroom cabin, some on cots, to see how a group would react, and then put three in each of the two remaining one-bedroom cabins. I had two friends who were helping me, and we would sleep in the lodge's common room on cots.

We had to be away from the kids so we could conduct the experiment, part of which was to record them as we projected various sounds from the forest using portable sound equipment. Looking back, it was kind of primitive, but it was the best I could come up with.

I wanted to record their reactions to hearing various sounds at night, as it was the only way I knew to see if they were frightened or not. Most of the sounds would be benign, but not all. They had no idea, of course, of what we were up to. They would also answer a questionnaire before the experiment began, as well as wear heart-rate monitors.

We had about an equal number of guys and gals, and after everyone arrived, we assigned them their cabins, telling them to come up to the main lodge for dinner where we'd talk about the experiment. The meals were catered as part of the cost, everyone eating cafeteria style.

After eating, we introduced ourselves, had them each get up and say a few words about themselves, then we basically just told them we wanted them to get a good night's sleep and would start the experiment in the morning after breakfast. The experiment would actually start that night, but we didn't want them to suspect anything.

It seemed like anytime we advertised for experiments, we would get mostly freshmen, with a few sophomores. I think this was because these younger kids were more excited about college, wanting to get involved in everything.

This bunch was the same way, almost entirely freshmen, so we were looking at more of a younger spectrum of college students. I intended to experiment with older students at some point, for I wondered if one learned to overcome their fears as they got older.

I was never able to test this, as I basically had to reevaluate the entire premise of my experiment, based on what we saw there at the resort—in other words, I basically abandoned it. My fellowship was over not long after that anyway, and I ended up getting a teaching position across the country.

Like I mentioned, one cabin had six kids and two had three kids. For each group, we'd selected one as a control subject. That person listened to the sounds on the tape beforehand and was there to help control what was going on, since we couldn't be in the cabins. (Note that I'm not using the term control subject like one would in an experimental or statistical sense, but only as a way to describe their role in trying to control the situation.)

We didn't want things going south on us, and the control subject was there to make sure nobody got too scared, as well as making sure the kids didn't turn on their iPads and stuff like that and thereby not even hear the sounds. Each control subject had been instructed to tell their cabin mates they were seasoned outdoors people, which would hopefully give them the credibility they needed when later identifying each sound.

Well, first of all, it didn't work like we'd hoped. Second, after this experiment, I had to change my entire view of everything, as you'll see.

What was on the tape? It started out with simple sounds of the forest, like owls and other birds, then gradually evolved to other sounds that were less likely to be identified, such as an elk in rut.

We had to be careful not to overdo it, or it would be obvious what was going on. The sounds had to be spread out over a good deal of time. One of the scarier sounds was of a bull walking along, making a growling noise, like they often do, but which you wouldn't know was a bull if you hadn't been around them.

Our control subjects were instructed to tell the students what each sound was after they'd all heard it to see if this knowledge lessened the heart rate the second time we'd play it. People tend to be somewhat afraid of sounds they aren't familiar with, but it's typically not that irrational fear you get when talking about big hairy monsters.

I don't know if you ever saw the movie, "The Boggy Creek Monster," but the scene with the monster at the bathroom window is what I'm talking about when I mention irrational fear. It's that same fear that makes horror movies what they are—we know deep inside these things don't exist, it's just a movie, yet we're scared to death anyway. This is the type of fear I was trying to study to see if it could be epigenetic.

So, the end of the tape had a couple of recordings I'd taken from the Internet of supposed Bigfoot encounters. I could compare the reactions the students had to the sounds they couldn't identify, yet were of real creatures, like the elk bugling and the bull, with these Bigfoot sounds, sounds of supposed big hairy monsters.

After playing the first Bigfoot sound, our control subjects were instructed to tell the students they were listening to a moose, then we would play the second Bigfoot call and see if they were still exhibiting irrational fear.

Like I said, it was a preliminary experiment, and I knew it was going to need some fine tuning, but I really didn't expect to have to completely abandon it. And since it was for only one night, I thought I'd get some good preliminary results to work with.

OK, hopefully that's enough background to give you an idea of what the setup was. So, here we were, deep in a Montana forest, only the walls of the cabins between us and the wilderness, messing around with something I later realized we really didn't understand, in more ways than one.

The control subjects had been instructed to engage the others in board games for the evening, and we'd start the recordings early, then gradually go to the scarier sounds when things were winding down and everyone was getting tired. They were also to be sure there was no talk of anything spooky.

My friends Jack and Diana were out in the woods, not too far from the cabins, manning the sound equipment, which we'd set up before the students showed up.

Jack and Diana later told me they'd been scared from the start, as the forest was very primal feeling after dark, and they'd immediately got the feeling they were being watched. The fact that they didn't abandon everything and come inside was a testament to their courage.

We found out later (much later) that all had gone well with the sounds, the control subjects telling everyone what each sound was, and though there'd been some concern about the bugling elk, no one had actually shown any fear until the bull sound, and even that was soon old hat, though a few were somewhat nervous at the thought of a big bull outside.

But there was none of that irrational fear until the first so-called Bigfoot sound was broadcast, and the kids had definitely been scared, not believing it was a moose looking for a mate.

That first sound was the less scary of the two, being mostly a grunt and loud growl, but the second was the infamous siren sound that Bigfoot supposedly makes, going on and on and on at a really loud volume. When that sound was played, the fears planted by the first Bigfoot sound came into full bloom, and everyone was scared stiff, many wanting to get in their cars and leave.

We'd instructed the control subjects to tell the kids what was going on if they seemed about to lose it, as we didn't want anyone leaving during the night.

But after the sound was over, the kids seemed to become rational again, deciding to stay. This was actually the end of the experiment, and we would spend the next day discussing how they'd felt, then everyone would go home that afternoon.

Jack and Diana now came inside the lodge, happy to be indoors, saying they'd felt really nervous out there. We all talked for awhile, then finally went to bed, tired. It was probably around one a.m. at that point.

Well, if you've read about any Bigfoot encounters, which I've read plenty of since this happened, you would probably guess that the calls somehow attracted the attention of Bigfoot, who then came to pay us a visit. I think that's exactly what happened, but not in the way you'd be inclined to think, with it looking through the windows or trying to get inside and scaring us.

That night, we all slept like rocks, with the cook waking us the next morning banging around in the kitchen, making blueberry pancakes for breakfast. We had to go wake the kids up, as they were all asleep. I was eager to talk to them and see how they described the previous night.

We had a good breakfast, then I gathered everyone around and asked how their night had gone. I told them I'd been told they'd heard lots of night sounds and asked them to tell me about them.

Well, I wasn't a bit prepared for what they told me. They described everything in detail, including the scary bull sound, but nobody mentioned the Bigfoot sounds at all, even when I asked if they'd heard anything else. Not a single one of them acted like they'd heard anything.

Had they caught on to the experiment and decided to try to trick us? It seemed unlikely, especially since the control people would have to be in on it, and there really was no motive for doing so.

No matter what I did, I couldn't get anyone to admit to having heard any Bigfoot sounds. Out of 12 people, not a single one said they'd heard anything after the bull sound.

I was shocked—were they all in denial, repressing what had been a frightening experience? I knew people did this, but all 12? It seemed preposterous to think that all of them would react like that, and repression of trauma was typically after something more serious, like a bad car accident or something truly horrific.

I took the three control subjects aside and questioned them in private, but they all seemed puzzled by what I wanted to know. Since these three were the only ones getting paid anything for their time at the experiment, I expected them to be forthcoming, but I finally had to admit no one had any remembrance of the sounds at all.

What a puzzler! I had, of course, heard them, both when played in the forest and before when I'd first recorded them, and I felt they were scary, but not to the point of outright repression. I'm not a psychologist, but it just didn't seem logical.

Later, when I got back and checked the heart-rate monitor read-outs, I could clearly see evidence that every single one of them had heard something scary, not once, but twice, which correlated to the experiment. It was strange, but I decided the experiment had measured something I hadn't anticipated. I needed to talk to some of my psychologist friends for their opinions.

But back to the lodge. Over breakfast, I noticed that everyone seemed unusually quiet, a big contrast to dinner the night before. In fact, they were all talking about leaving, and it wasn't long before they'd all done exactly that. The resort had some fun things to do, nothing totally exciting, but I'd expected them to stick around for the day and enjoy the beautiful creekside setting, playing horseshoes, badminton, or even just relaxing. But it just seemed like they couldn't wait to leave, and to be honest, my friends Jack and Diana seemed to feel the same way.

Since we'd all come separately, I was the last to leave, checking through the cabins to make sure no one had left anything, then locking it all up and dropping the key in the mailbox slot of the lodge.

I then realized Jack and Diana had left the recording equipment out in the woods, so I went to retrieve it. I remember seeing lots of large tracks all around the equipment, though it didn't appear to have been bothered. I gathered it up, then headed back for the lodge, which wasn't more than 100 feet away.

And the next thing I recall, I was waking, leaning against a tree, and it was dark, cold, and raining—and I was thoroughly soaked.

It was September, and being in northern Montana, the snows can come anytime. The weather forecast hadn't called for anything severe, but there I was, alone and soaking wet, and I no longer even had the key to the lodge to get inside and get warmed up.

But no matter, all my stuff was in my car, and I needed to get home anyway, especially before it started snowing, which it felt cold enough to do any minute. The recording equipment was soaked.

I fumbled though my pockets for my keys, wondering how and why I'd gone to sleep like that. It was something I wouldn't normally have done in a million years. And I had the most bizarre disoriented feeling, like I'd been drinking, though I don't drink. I can't even describe it, it was such a foreign feeling.

My sense of balance was off, is the only way I can think of to describe how it felt. You know how you feel when you wake up and aren't sure where you are, maybe you've had a strange dream? It was like that, but completely overpowering to the point I'm lucky I was able to even find my car and get out of the cold rain.

I started the car and sat there for the longest time, trying to reorient myself and get warm. Finally, from nowhere, I had the urge to get out of there as fast as I could, as if something was coming, something very primal and threatening.

It was then that I experienced that irrational fear I'd been studying, and I have to say it was a first for me. I was suddenly panicked, and my life felt like it was on the line in the worst possible way. I started shaking, even though by then the heater had pretty much warmed me up, and I punched the door lock button, put it in gear, and started up the lodge's long driveway, the same one I'd thought was so pretty when I'd first come there, the way it wound through tall trees. Now, in the dark and mud, the drive looked impassable, and the trees felt menacing, what I could make of them.

I was halfway up the drive when I suddenly blanked out—not physically, but mentally. I had no idea who I was, where I was, or why I was there. I didn't even know why I was driving up the road, and my inclination was to stop and try to figure it all out.

As I slowed the car, I realized how muddy the road was, and I knew if I didn't keep going I would be stuck, and yet I somehow needed to stop. And at this point, I have to say my brain was in deep conflict with something, maybe my subconscious, that something that keeps us alive at an instinctual, maybe even epigenetic, level.

Fortunately, my instincts won out, or I might not be here to tell you this story, for as I started accelerating, sliding around in the mud, I caught a glimpse in my taillights of two glowing red eyes coming up behind me at a fast pace, and I somehow knew, again instinctively, that it was one of the big hairy monsters I'd thought were long gone in the deep past of human history, only living on in our genetic memories.

This was no memory, but was alive and well, and it quickly caught up to my car, stepping up onto my rear bumper and crawling onto the roof, even as I began going faster and faster. For some reason, the fear it brought with it made me more aware of who I was, and I regained my sense of reality and why I was there.

I could definitely feel the extra weight on the car as it slowed a little, the roof even sagging in some above me, making me wonder how long it would hold up to what must be a lot of weight.

I soon had the car going pretty fast, and as I made the turn onto the main road, I felt the thing slip off, and I saw it again running behind me, unable to catch up. I don't even recall the drive home, even though it took two hours, for I felt as if I'd seen into a different world, one that I'd thought was long gone. How could it be that these things were still with us? Had I imagined it all? I would've preferred to believe that, but the deep and long scratch marks I found on my car's roof and trunk the next day led me to believe otherwise.

I spent the next few days pretty much holed up in my house, trying to make sense of what had happened. If the creature was malevolent and had wished me harm, why not do something while I'd been asleep and defenseless? And why had I gone to sleep like that? It almost felt like I'd been drugged, and it actually took several days to feel normal again.

Just what had made the kids all forget the Bigfoot sounds they'd heard? Was it an innate defense mechanism, or had it been some kind of strange outside influence? After what I'd experienced, my vote was for the latter explanation. I've since read that some believe Bigfoot has the ability to mess with one's mind, but it just doesn't make sense, though I know there's a lot we don't understand.

The real question for me, though, was this: Had other things gone on that night that none of us remembered? The thought gave me the chills.

Well, it wasn't long before I started hearing back from some of my guinea pigs, so to speak. Some of them had started recalling things, and they'd gotten together to compare notes and found their stories matched. They wanted to know if I'd engineered these things, and if so, why? A few were even angry with me, saying they hadn't signed up to be traumatized.

I decided it would be good to try and gather everyone together to talk about things, though I was the last to want to do so. I preferred to just forget the whole thing, as it left me feeling like things were out of my control and I'd failed everyone. But I at least knew to get someone more knowledgeable involved, so I recruited a psychologist friend, the very same one who'd helped me design the experiment in the first place.

We all met in a conference room on campus, and what followed was mystifying and yet predictable, at least in my mind.

Everyone talked about the entire night being so frightening that they'd had trouble later with nightmares and such, and yet no one could actually verbalize what had happened, if anything. It seemed to have just been a night of fears running amok, and yet something had triggered it. We never did get to the source of anything, nor did anyone actually recount seeing or hearing anything. It just seemed like everyone had this deep irrational fear, the kind I'd been wanting to study and yet didn't know how to quantify or deal with it. I think everyone left the session feeling better for having discussed it, yet nothing was different.

I knew the creature had been real, but I'd decided not to further worry anyone. I'd seen it, and I now knew the meaning of trauma at a gut level. I wanted nothing more to do with the subject, hopefully being able to someday forget it.

Had the students actually dealt with a Bigfoot or had it just been a case of primal and perhaps epigenetic fears running wild, maybe reinforced by the setting, one another, and the Bigfoot recordings?

I'll never know. I thought about going back to that resort for a gut check, but I knew it was something I couldn't do, especially alone, which I would need to be. I read not too long after that it had been closed down, but there was no mention of why. I have actually driven by it a couple of times, as it's on the way to the Canadian border and I used to go visit Canada once in awhile as it was so close, but that's all been years ago.

Did we humans once fear big hairy monsters? Well, if you look at some of the fossils from the Pleistocene, you'll see dire wolves, dire bears, and all kinds of fearsome creatures, but I have yet to see a fossil of anything like Bigfoot.

Those Pleistocene creatures are all extinct now, but I personally know that Bigfoot isn't, though I must say I would sleep better knowing it was, though I know it's not good to wish that on any species.

6

THOSE THINGS WE CAN'T KNOW

Larry and I met at the Museum of the Rockies in Bozeman, where they were having a display of Montana dinosaurs. I was spending some time in that area helping my friend wth his fly-fishing business, and my wife, Sarah, who was still in Colorado, made me promise to go to the exhibit. As a geologist, she was interested in what news was coming from one of the premier dinosaur collecting regions in the world.

I personally don't know much about the giant beasts, and I will say the talk was interesting, but not nearly as intriguing as the story my new friend told me later over lunch downtown. —Rusty

I'm a teacher in a small town in eastern Montana, and my hobby used to be fossils and paleontology. This may sound like an odd hobby, but I live near one of the most famous dig sites in the world of dinosaurs—Hell Creek. It may not be well-known to the world in general, but to paleontologists, it's one of the creme de la creme of dinosaur fossil sites.

Montana has a lot of dinosaurs, and Hell Creek is one of the best places to find them. It's the home of T. Rex—over 25 percent of the fossils there are from that scary creature, which is found only in the western United States.

But let me tell you, there are other things buried in the badland sediments out there, things not yet catalogued by paleontologists or anyone else, things that scare me much more than the thought of a T. Rex, for who knows if they're still around or not?

Let me give you some background. It all started with our school principal leaving a flyer on my desk from a famous museum in the Midwest announcing its summer field season exploring the nearby Hell Creek Formation, inviting teachers to volunteer. It was an opportunity to see how paleontology really worked and thereby enrich our high-school students' educations in the sciences.

What was not to like? I could work alongside professionals, learning about how fossils were excavated and analyzed. I'd been fascinated by Hell Creek for years, but had never had this kind of an opportunity, my experience mostly being just driving around the area and doing a little exploration of the badlands on my own. I'd actually found a few T. Rex teeth, which I'd been told were really common there, but nothing else, unless snakes and mosquitoes count. So, I sent in my application.

Let me tell you a little about Hell Creek in case you're not familiar with it. It was once a small tributary of the Missouri River in northeastern Montana, but is now a flooded arm of Fort Peck Reservoir and part of the Charles M. Russell National Wildlife Refuge.

If you go north of the little town of Jordan—population maybe 250 and the largest town in Garfield County—you can take a grueling washboard road to Hell Creek State Park on the shores of the lake. This is the center of Hell Creek, and the official Hell Creek Fossil Area is nearby.

You would think that, being a state park on the shores of a big lake, it would be a pleasant place, but in the summer it's literally hell —mosquitoes, unbearable heat, and monotonous-looking rock bluffs that stretch as far as you can see. And of course, summer is when the surveys and digs take place, primarily because everyone has school the rest of the year, whether student or teacher. Plus the winters are too treacherous, windy, and unbearably cold.

The Hell Creek Formation stretches for miles and miles, the first T. Rex having been found over a hundred miles south of the actual creek in 1902. The rocks are like a red, orange, tan, and black layer cake, badlands laid down 67 or so million years ago, right at the end of the dinosaur dynasty before they were all killed off by the Yucatan asteroid.

It's a veritable dinosaur graveyard, and thereby a popular place to search. And there have been some major finds there, like the teenaged T. Rex named Jane (for a museum donor) and a whole pack of Triceratops, the three-horned arch-nemesis of T. Rex, which had formerly been thought to be a solitary non-pack animal.

And yes, the Triceratops was a good match for the T. Rex, as its horns made it quite lethal, even though it was a herbivore. The first Triceratops found there was named Homer, for the Simpsons, and it's estimated that around 40 percent of the fossils found so far in Hell Creek are of this animal.

OK, I could go on and on about dinosaurs, but that's not what this is really about, as you'll eventually see if you'll bear with me. And though the Hell Creek area is one big dino graveyard, I found it had another kind of creature buried there, one not really as well known to science as the dinosaurs, which surprises me, since I don't think it's extinct but is a living creature—well, not the ones I found, but you know what I mean.

One would think the museum would concentrate its efforts around the actual Hell Creek area, but this season, they'd decided to explore more out in the outlier part of the formation, which was an area near the small town of Ekalaka, population 300, near the state line where Montana meets the Dakotas.

Ekalaka got its name from a Sioux woman who married the town's founder, and means *restless* or *moving about*. It's part of the Montana Dinosaur Trail and has a museum known for its dinosaur collection. The town's near where Jane had been discovered, as well as Homer and his pack.

Ekalaka sits near Custer National Forest, an oasis of cool pine forest above the badlands, and the museum had rented out a collection of large cabins there called Camp Needmore. It was the same place where the paleontologists who'd discovered Homer had stayed, so we hoped we were following in their tradition and would find something significant.

Fossil hunting is far from glamorous and is more like a form of self torture, at least in Hell Creek. Basically, it just amounts to looking for something different. A fossil can typically be something like a brown bulge sticking out of tan-colored rocks.

We call it prospecting, and basically you end up just walking up-and-down the coulees, deep ravines eroded into the landscape by the occasional rains. The secret is to look for scraps of bone that have washed down, then follow them back up to their source.

Sometimes all you find are scraps, but these can lead you to an important bone bed. So, basically you just spend most of your time wandering up and down ravines, trying to keep hydrated and fighting off various biting flies and mosquitoes.

Part of the deal is that you take notes, so your efforts aren't replicated needlessly by other wanderers or prospectors. I found that drawing rough maps really helps, but we also each had a GPS.

Sometimes you just stumble upon a fragment of a skeleton, but if you're lucky, you may find a whole one. In any case, it's exciting to find something that's been buried for millions of years. If you do happen to find something, you may dig a little into the bank to see what's there, and if it looks promising, it's the job of the trip leader or paleontologist to decide whether the prospect is worth excavating.

We would occasionally find places where bone pirates had dug, which is extremely illegal. These people will search for dinosaur bones and sell them on the black market, which removes them from scientific study.

Anyway, there I was, my first formal prospecting trip, and I was really excited. The project head was a paleontologist named Dave, who was from this famous museum, a really well-known guy and a joy to work with, and his sidekick was another paleontologist named

Gerry who taught at a university. The rest of the project members were mostly grad students from an assortment of places, and there were several of us teacher volunteers.

The first night they had a chili dinner around a campfire, and I can say the atmosphere was supercharged with excitement. Many of the students had never been in the West before, especially in a place as famous as Hell Creek. The high-school teachers were a more sedate bunch, and if I recall correctly, we were all from Montana, so were a bit more jaded about the landscape.

That night was a little irritating for me, for the kids in the cabin next to mine seemed to be up all night partying. I guess I'm an old codger, 'cause it kept me awake. But as I lay there, I recall thinking about how extensive the Hell Creek Formation was, and how it had captured in its layers a time so totally different from my own, a time when dinosaurs ruled these badlands, though back then they were swamps fed by large meandering rivers. It was mysterious to me, and it seemed that, no matter how many bones we dug up and studied, there were many things we would never know.

The next day we were up early, having breakfast and coffee, then we split into teams and headed out into the miles of monotonous badlands around Ekalaka, trying to get out before the heat became unbearable. It was only 8:30 in the morning, but the temperature was already 83 degrees. It broke 100 every day I was there.

I was teamed with a group of three students who had been out here before, two guys and a gal from somewhere in Indiana. They were pros and, even though I was much older, I was to follow their lead. I didn't say much, as I'd spent years wandering similar badlands near the town I taught in and was pretty adept at taking care of myself.

We were soon bouncing in an SUV down a two-track that barely qualified as a road, heading out into a part of a grid that on the map had looked flat and easy, but was really an impossible mess of draws and coulees and cliffs.

The sky was a bluebird blue, but I could see some clouds forming far to the west, and my badlands experience said it was probably going to rain that afternoon, which would turn the nice firm road we were on into a muddy mess. I suspected that the rest of my crew had no idea what might be coming, so it would be up to me to make sure we all got out before a big thunderstorm hit.

It didn't take long for the two-track to end at the head of a draw that looked impossible to access, but I was with an intrepid bunch who soon found a way down. We immediately found a bunch of teeth that one of the students said was from a pony-sized animal called a Troodon, a close relative of larger omnivorous raptors also found in the area.

The rest of the day came up pretty empty handed, except for, of course, a number of T. Rex teeth. We followed the wash where we'd found them back to its source, but found no bones. I figured the T. Rex itself had either long ago washed away while exposed to the elements or was still buried back deep in the layers at the head of the wash.

The clouds had indeed built up and were looking threatening when we finally found our way back to our SUV and headed back out, barely reaching pavement before the deluge started. We found out when we reached our camp that several rigs hadn't yet returned and were presumably stuck.

There was nothing we could do about that, so we went into our respective cabins and got cleaned up, hoping dinner wouldn't be delayed, which of course it was.

Eventually everyone returned, we had dinner, then sat around and examined what everyone had found, the experts among us trying to determine exactly what each fossil was. A few merited further examination, and several of the groups would be going back to the sites where they'd been.

Well, when out in the badlands, it's a good rule of thumb to stick together, for a sprained ankle, snakebite, or even a broken limb were definitely possibilities and could be fatal if there was no one there to help you. But I've always been a loner, and I found that I was much better at prospecting when alone with nobody around to distract me. So, after spending several days with the same group of students, I found myself yearning for the isolation and solitude that had drawn me to the area in the first place.

It was another hot day, but this time we were on a better access road, stopping near a ridge high above the Hell Creek Formation. We would have to make our way down some distance to be where we wanted, and in the process of making my way around numerous cliffs and draws, I became separated from the rest of the group.

I had a rough idea where they were, but my natural inclination towards being alone took over, and I headed towards the soft grays and gray greens of the Hell Creek, but in a different direction. I would search on my own, and the odds would thereby be better that I would find something. Or at least so I thought.

I slowly slid into a small drainage, the soft clays breaking my speed and sending small avalanches ahead of me. And bingo, right there at my feet was my first fossil! It had been too easy, but was it anything worthwhile or just another T. Rex tooth?

I picked it up and examined it. I had no idea what I was looking at, but it looked like some kind of very large toe. Was it even a fossil? I wasn't sure, as it didn't have the hardness one would expect, nor did the cellular structure have that hard smooth but knobby feel that dino bones have. Fossilization is basically the replacement of cells by minerals, and this almost looked like a more recent animal bone.

I stuck it in my pocket, then started looking up the wash I'd slid down into, scanning the ground carefully as I worked my way upstream. It then dawned on me that I was still far above the Hell Creek and in a younger formation that I wasn't that familiar with. Was it the Fox Hills? I wasn't even sure what formations were above and below the Hell Creek.

As I worked my way up the coulee, I found yet another bone, but this was a tooth, a large molar, much larger than a human's, but similar looking.

I was perplexed. What animal had teeth like these? Had I stumbled into an area of more recent animals, maybe even something Pleistocene? Or was I simply looking at the bones from a large herbivore like a cow? It didn't look fossilized either, but I stuck it in my pocket with the other bone.

Now, part of the deal was that we all carried radios, and that was part of why I wasn't too worried about getting separated from everyone. I got a call saying everyone was meeting back at the SUV and where was I? I told them I would be back muy pronto, took a GPS reading of the spot I was at, and headed back. The heat was so oppressive I was ready to go anyway, even though I'd hoped to get to the head of the wash and see what else might be there.

On the way back, I found the fossilized fragments of a turtle shell, a crocodile vertebra, and a number of small pieces of bone, but nothing of real interest.

Later, back at camp, I showed one of the paleontologists, Dave, what I'd found. He examined it closely, then said he thought it might be a foot bone from a human-sized therapod called an oviraptosaur, which were weird toothless dinosaurs with crests of bone on their skulls. I then showed him the tooth, and he seemed puzzled.

"I don't think this is a fossil at all, nor is the toe you showed me, the more I look at it. They both have enough deposit in them that I at first thought they might be from stream-channel sands that hardened into a weak sandstone, but now I don't think that's the case. Do you mind if I show them to Gerry?"

Gerry was the other paleontologist at the site. I gave the pieces to Dave and headed back to my cabin, hoping the next-door students were quieter that night. Not too long after, both Dave and Gerry came over, asking me where I'd found the bones.

I took out my GPS and showed them the coordinates, which they copied down. They then asked me if I would go out there with them the next day, which I agreed to.

Now, you may know more about the topic than I do, which wouldn't be hard to do, but I do know that paleontologists have to take a lot of classes in anatomy, not just of humans, but of all kinds of critters.

In fact, some paleontologists serve as a kind of bone expert for their communities, identifying all sorts of weird and strange stuff brought to them by the locals, which typically end up being skunk skulls, raccoon toes, and things like that. These guys are pretty knowledgeable about bones of all kinds. They're kind of the forensic anthropologists of the animal world.

So, when these two guys told me they had no idea what they were looking at, but they knew it was no cow or horse, I was surprised. They did know the bones were definitely not fossilized and were probably less than 50 years old, depending on how much they'd been out in the weather.

We talked some about where I'd found them, made plans for the next day, then they left, and I went to bed, tired. That night, a huge thunderstorm moved in, the kind that fills the coulees with dangerous flash-flood waters, and I knew nobody would be going anywhere the next day, for everything would be a sticky gumbo.

Sure enough, the next day was spent in camp, which I don't think anyone minded one bit, as none of us were really used to long hot days of hiking through coulees and washes.

It was nice to be in the cool pines, and the humidity from the storm passing through made it balmy and pleasant. The bones I'd found were making the rounds, everyone trying to figure out what they could be, studying the geological maps for what formation they'd come from and such and whatnot.

Me, I spent most of the day reading, gave my wife a call, and just lazed about in general.

The next day dawned clear and even a bit chilly from the passing storm. After breakfast, I was informed by Dave that he and Gerry wouldn't be going out with me that day after all, as someone had found something that looked like it could be an intact Edmontosaurus, the third most common dinosaur in the Hell Creek, a plant eater that weighed in at seven tons and was forty feet long.

They were excited and invited me along, but I wanted to go back and check out the rest of the wash where I'd found the two bones. They wished me well and said they still hoped to get out there before the survey was over.

I was soon back in the wash, my comrades exploring down lower in another coulee. Now at the spot where I'd found the tooth, I slowly walked up the wash, which was getting tighter and steeper.

Holy cow! There it was, yet another tooth, even bigger than the other! I continued upwards, now huffing and puffing up the steep slope, finally stopping to catch my breath. And what I saw before me made my senses reel!

There, sticking out from the edge of the wash were more bones, but these were huge, real bones, not like a toe or tooth, but more like femurs and shoulder bones and bones I didn't even know the names of.

I pulled myself up next to where they stuck out of the dirt, trying to examine them more closely. A lower arm bone stuck out, and it was at least three times the size of mine! And there was what looked like a vertebra, as big as my hand! And so many bones! I knew I was looking at the remnants of at least four or five individuals, if not more.

Was I looking at some kind of burial ground? And what was it, some kind of large hominid? I'm not really religious, but I immediately thought of the giants of the Bible and wondered if I hadn't found some kind of prehistoric race of ancient people. If so, it would propel my name to the top of the news literally overnight.

I caught my breath, then pulled myself up closer. Now I was next to what looked like a large femur, and it looked very much like it had been scraped with something sharp. That was odd!

I leaned back, not sure what to do. My first thought was to head back to the SUV, radio the others, then go tell Dave and Gerry about my find. Surely it would top any Edmontosaurus, the discovery of a race of huge hominids or whatever they were. But maybe I should look around more. After all, it was still early, and the others wouldn't be wanting to go back to camp this soon.

The coulee had tightened to where I could no longer walk up it, so I backtracked a ways and climbed out as soon as I could, walking back around to its head. I was astounded by what I found, my earlier findings paling in comparison.

I was shocked, to say the least, for before me lay an entire bleached-out bonefield, perhaps with twenty or more skeletons, though it was hard to say, as they were scattered, some half-buried, others sticking only slightly out of the dirt.

I was mesmerized, and yet I felt sick. I had to be looking at some kind of battlefield or even a massacre. All the bones looked as if they'd been hacked by knives or something sharp, many broken and scattered. But as I walked towards the sight, almost involuntarily, what I made out next was beyond belief.

Here and there, scattered with the rest of the bones, were skulls —huge skulls with thick brows that looked almost human, with blocky jaws. But many were smashed in as if having taken blows from something large and heavy, and in some cases, the teeth were missing completely, even the jaws. I was looking at something beyond my comprehension, at something I could never know or understand.

I felt a sudden compulsion to get away as fast as I could. I ran back to the coulee and headed down, down, down, barely looking where I was going, panicked like I've never been before, sliding out of control.

Finally at the bottom, I started back up the ridge to the SUV, still feeling as if I was being chased by some strange force from another world. Once on top, I looked back in the direction of the bones, shivering, and was soon on the radio with my colleagues, telling them I had to leave soon as I was sick.

They came back, taking me to the cabins, concerned. I quickly packed up my stuff and said I was going home, and they asked me to call when I got there, worried, but I told them I would be OK, it was just the heat and I needed to back off and stay inside for awhile.

Dave called me at home that evening to see if I was OK, and I told him the same story about it being the heat, and he seemed satisfied with that, expressing concern and telling me to come back anytime. But I knew I was never going back there—in fact, I was never going to do any more prospecting anywhere.

I've thought about what I saw that day many times, wondering what it was, what had actually happened. Was it a battle between their own kind, or had humans taken it upon themselves to do them in? And why had I felt an uncontrollable urge to flee?

I would never know, and there are some things we don't need to know, I guess, for thinking about them is not a good thing.

I had intended to tell Dave and Gerry about my find later, but I just never got around to it. I kept the GPS coordinates for a long time, then finally threw them away, knowing I never wanted to go back.

Perhaps it was a significant find—actually, I know it was, so why not report it? I can't answer that question, except to say maybe it had something to do with respect for the dead. But to be honest, no, that wasn't it, it was just the sheer terror of seeing something so removed from the things I knew.

It felt like one of those things we can't know because to know it would be too terrifying.

7

DON'T FEED THE WILDLIFE

Fittingly enough, I met Monty and his wife Trish at a fruit stand in the little Western Colorado town of Palisade. I say fittingly, as they have a cherry orchard near Flathead Lake in Montana. Palisade is part of Colorado's fruit-growing region, famous for its peaches, but one can also buy cherries there. The couple was on vacation, sampling the wares of other fruit growers and generally enjoying themselves. My wife Sarah and I had made the trip to stock up on fruit to freeze and can for the winter.

Well, as it usually does, one thing led to another, and we ended up inviting them to stop in our hometown of Steamboat Springs on their way back home, which they did. They came to the fly-fishing clinic I was holding that day, then told me this story over a delicious trout dinner Sarah cooked up that night out at our little cabin. —Rusty

My wife Trish and I own a cherry orchard on the shores of Flathead Lake near the small town of Bigfork, Montana, just south of Kalispell.

I don't know if you know that area, but Flathead Lake is the largest freshwater lake west of the Mississippi, and the region has a fairly mild climate with warm days and crisp cool nights, which helps set the sugars in the fruit. Since it's fairly far north, the days are long in the summer.

This makes conditions perfect for orchards like mine, as well as for vineyards and wineries. There are also peaches, plums, apples, and pears grown there, but the cherries are king and are famous, as is the cherry wine.

Let me point out that the lake is less than an hour's drive to Glacier National Park, where I've heard of strange going-ons for years through the grapevine. The park employees will tell you you're nuts if you mention these things, but if you ask those who live near the park, like the residents of the small town of Hungry Horse, you'll get a different story. I know people who used to fish at Hungry Horse Reservoir who won't go near the place any more.

Also keep in mind that Flathead Lake is near both the Bob Marshall Wilderness and the Great Bear Wilderness, as well as several mountain ranges, and that's just to the east. West of the lake is rugged country, too, and lots of it. There's plenty of room for Bigfoot out there, which is what I'm talking about.

Now, there's also a legend about the Flathead Monster, Flessie, who supposedly lives in the lake. Even though the lake is over 300 feet deep in places, I think the monster is just the result of overactive imaginations. But Bigfoot? Well, some may say the same about it, but I personally know better. Let me tell you why.

Our property isn't one of the larger orchards in the area, and for us, it's kind of more a hobby than an income producer, as I'm a retired contractor. I hire a couple of people to help out during the busy season, but most of the time, Trish and I do everything ourselves, even though we're getting older and starting to slow down.

Well, there's a reason we bought the cherry orchard beyond wanting to raise cherries. It's actually one of the older places on the lake and has a beautiful bungalow that was one of the first houses around. My wife loves it, and she's basically restored it, along with some help from me.

It sits on a small hill just above the orchards, and you can see the lake below. In May, it's one of the most beautiful sights you'll ever see

—the blues of the lake behind masses of fluffy pinkish-white cherry blossoms with snowcapped peaks in the distance. By July the tree branches are heavy with glistening red fruit.

It's all very pastoral, and we love it. And our place isn't far from the docks at Woods Bay, where we can put in with our boat and go fishing or just cruising. Our kids are all grown, but they all live within an hour or two and come visit to go waterskiing.

All in all, it's a great place to live, beautiful and peaceful, and yet near the large town of Kalispell and places like Glacier. After we moved there from Missoula, we had lots of friends wanting to come stay. Missoula's an OK town, but it seems like it's always smoked in for the summer and gray in the winter, partly because it sits in a bowl.

My wife, Trish, really got into the rural lifestyle when we moved, after being cooped up in a subdivision, and the place has a small barn, so she went out and got some chickens for eggs. Since there's a fenced pasture, the chickens can free range there, then at night they go roost in the barn. It's great, as we have fresh eggs all the time, and they're pretty easy to care for.

We do have predators around, mostly foxes and coyotes, and once in a blue moon a black bear will wander through, mostly in late summer and fall when things are ripe, because of all the orchards around.

There are grizzlies in the area, but they generally stay in the back-country. They have been seen in some of the state parks that are found around the lakeshore, but that's because they can smell the trash, though everything's pretty much bear proof and they get hazed away, or even trapped and relocated.

My wife's an animal lover, and she got to where she named each chicken and pretty much turned them into pets. They would come running when they'd see her and follow her around. She was very conscientious about making sure they were all in and safe at night and even had me install a monitor in the barn so she could check on them.

Well, we were very happy, living the pastoral life, until something odd happened. You won't read about it in any paper, but if you get on social media, you might be able to still find some comments, even though it's now been a good five years back.

It all started with the neighbor down the road from us. He called one day to let us know that someone or something had broken into his feed shed where he kept the grain and tack for his two horses. We have kind of a neighborhood alert system, though normally one wouldn't call the neighbors about something so minor, but he was concerned, even though his tack hadn't been stolen.

Whatever it was, they'd pretty much broken down the door, taken over 20 pounds of cracked corn from a big metal container, and scattered things around. He couldn't figure out what they'd been looking for, but he called the sheriff anyway and reported it. He also said his horses were spooked and wouldn't go out in the pasture the next morning.

Something like that makes you want to batten down the hatches, yet it's not really that concerning, as it seems pretty minor in the grand scheme of things. Given what he'd said, I just figured it was a black bear, and they're typically pretty shy. I didn't expect any trouble, as it probably had already discovered the nearby state park and was over there looking for garbage, which is where most of the bears end up, like I mentioned.

Well, after a day or so, the incident was forgotten and we all went about our business. It was early August, and the main cherry harvest had begun, the busiest time of year for the growers.

We grow primarily Sweethearts, a large heart-shaped cherry that doesn't ripen until mid-August, so we're not as deep into harvest in early August as are those who grow Rainiers or Lapins. And we sell a lot of our cherries to roadside stands, so we don't have to worry about boxing and shipping like some do.

Like I said, this is more of a hobby for us as opposed to a business, so we don't typically get as stressed that time of year as do a lot of the growers who depend on the money. I mention this because I think the stress added to what happened, making it much worse.

Well, it wasn't but a few days later when someone down the road from the first guy reported something broke into their root cellar where they'd stored a bunch of potatoes. Nothing was gone, but it appeared that whatever it was had rifled through the raw spuds, though nothing was taken or damaged.

But what was weird is that the guy's dogs had been barking, and he'd gotten up to see why and spotted what looked like a really tall skinny bear running down the road—on two legs. It left him feeling uncomfortable, he'd said, because he didn't think it was a bear, but maybe a really big man. He couldn't understand why someone would try to eat raw potatoes and yet ignore the several dozen jars of canned fruit, tomatoes, and beets also stored there.

Well, these kind of things started happening on a daily basis all up and down the lake, from Bigfork clear down to Polson. It seems that whatever it was would work its way south, then come back north, taking several days to make the trip.

It didn't stay in one area too long, as if it knew it would get caught —or worse. A number of growers were ready to shoot it after it had gotten into their cherries and other fruits, even though it didn't do much damage, just apparently eating enough for each night's meal. For some reason, it stayed away from the West Shore, maybe because there aren't as many orchards

One night, it got into a roadside stand not too far from our place, putting us on high alert. By then, we'd finished our harvest and sold most of our fruit, but we still had several dozen boxes stored in the barn, waiting to be picked up by a winery on the West Shore. The cherries were stored in a small room so the chickens couldn't get into them, along with the chicken feed.

Rumors as to what this thing was had come fast and furious, and the general consensus was that it was a skinny sickly bear unable to feed itself in the forest, though we figured it had to have put on a lot of weight from all its foraging around the lakeshore. The few people who had seen it said it didn't look that much like a bear, as it was always upright, but nobody knew what else it could be.

Like most people around the lake, we also have dogs, two mutts we'd gotten at the shelter, though one has since passed from old age.

They both kind of looked like mixes between Australian Shepherds and Border Collies, smart as whips and very loyal.

These dogs had the run of the place during the day, but we always brought them in at night. We worried about them being outside at night, primarily because of bears and an occasional coyote—oh, and skunks.

The dogs seemed to have a sixth sense, knowing if there was anything outside, and would whine and bark, alerting us. I can't tell you how many times they'd bark and carry on and we'd go turn on the outside lights to see deer in the yard—they would bark at about anything. Well, except whatever it was making the rounds, and the night it came to visit us, these brave dogs went and hid under the bed.

I noticed they were acting strange, first pacing around and panting, then hiding, and I told Trish there was something odd going on. She immediately went and turned on all the outside lights. She'd caught it unawares and it ran away, ducking through the orchard and on down to the lake, according to the tracks we found the next day, though we hadn't seen it.

I found the tracks while out walking the dogs, and I'll have to admit they scared the you know what out of me, as well as the dogs, who started actually shaking. These were not bear tracks, not even close, but were larger than my own by a factor of at least two and were long and narrow, more like a human's than a bear's.

When I found them, I took the dogs back inside, got Trish and my camera and my shotgun, and we tracked them all the way down to the edge of the lake, where they disappeared into the water. We walked all up and down the shore, but never found more. It was if it had swam away. I thought about it later, and Flathead Lake has a number of small islands, so maybe it swam out to one.

We were both upset by this and were soon on the grapevine, talking to other neighbors about what we'd found. It turns out we weren't the only ones, and one woman had actually seen it duck down into the water, though it was dark enough she really couldn't make out what it was.

By then, rumors were making the rounds that it was Flessie, the

Flathead Lake Monster, named after the Loch Ness Monster, Nessie, though few could figure out how a water monster could sprout legs and start eating things like grain and vegetables from gardens and cherries.

As for Flessie, local tales go back more than 100 years, and there are still a couple of sightings each year, though in 1993, there were thirteen reports. One local story told how a little three-year-old boy fell into the lake and told his mom that the monster had lifted him up, saving him from drowning.

But Flessie looks nothing like what we were dealing with, as it's been described as a large eel-shaped creature that's twenty to forty feet long. Flathead Lake does have sturgeon, the largest ever caught being over seven feet long, so most of us figured that was the source of the legends.

In any case, we'd had a visit from something, and now Trish was worried about it getting the chickens. After seeing the tracks, she wanted to bring them into our basement, but knowing how messy they were, we didn't know how to accomplish that and still keep our house habitable. Trish proposed getting some cages for them, but we never did.

We left all the outside lights on, made sure the barn door was locked, then finally went to bed after taking the dogs out for a few minutes. They seemed fine, so we hoped the creature was gone. Trish had moved the monitor to our bedroom and kept watching the chickens, who were mostly just roosting at that point, in spite of the light in the barn we'd left on.

I wasn't as attached to the birds, but Trish's concern and worries made me feel bad, and I couldn't sleep. These silly birds had turned out to be much smarter than I would've ever guessed, and they treated Trish like a goddess, following her around and even trying to come inside with her. They would even come and sit on the windowsill by the TV room, apparently watching TV, and she got to where she'd leave it on with the sound off, just for them. I got to where I enjoyed their silly antics.

Trish had finally drifted off, and I'd finally decided I would get an electric hotwire the next day at the co-op and put it around the barn. That would surely keep an intruder out.

I was figuring out the logistics, lying there in bed, when the dogs jumped off and hid. I knew immediately our intruder was back.

I watched the monitor, wondering if it would go into the barn, wondering what I would do if it went after the chickens. I decided I should get up and get dressed, get my shotgun, and be prepared, as lying in bed sure wouldn't get the job done, whatever the job ended up being.

I decided not to wake Trish, so I quietly got up, grabbed my clothes, and dressed in the bathroom, then got my shotgun and looked out the window into the darkness. It took my eyes awhile to get acclimated, but I could eventually see something standing by the house, down almost to the back door.

Now my senses started to tingle, for what I saw was very strange. There was something big standing there, a big black blob, and it would light up like electricity was bouncing off it, like a small strobe light was hitting it, over and over. I could see its eyes shining in the flickering lights, as well as its dark fur and the outline of its limbs, its arms going way down almost to its knees. I couldn't really make out much else, even though the lights kept reflecting off it, but at a very low level, a blue-white color, very erratic.

I was both scared and puzzled. Was this thing somehow putting off an electrical charge? If so, my idea of an electrical fence probably wouldn't even faze it. I laughed at myself later, as I was always the practical contractor type, no matter what was going on, trying to figure out solutions.

I didn't know what to do and just stood there, frozen. But it gradually dawned on me that Trish had left the TV on, and this thing was watching it. It seemed mesmerized, and the flickering light shining off its eyes and coat was simply the light from the TV, nothing unusual, as eerie as it had seemed.

OK, so this thing had no special electrical powers, but it was still standing in our yard, looking into our window, and its reputation as a forager had included being destructive to gardens, root cellars, storage rooms, fruit stands—well, the list went on and on. I had to get rid of it somehow, and yet I didn't want to shoot it.

And it was big—how did I know I wouldn't make it angry and it would somehow come after me? As far as I knew, it hadn't gone into anyone's house yet, but it looked very capable of breaking into about anything it wanted.

I decided to stay put and watch it and see what it did. It stood there for the longest time, watching that darn TV, then finally, it put its arms up to the window as if to touch it.

It was then that I could make out its hands in the light, and it was a strange feeling to see they looked just like my own hands did, except much larger, of course. But this darn thing had thumbs. No wonder it was able to get into things like storage rooms and eat all the grain.

Now it backed up, looking puzzled, then turned and left. I was relieved—would it go back down to the lake? I hoped so, as I had no idea how to deal with it.

But no, instead, it went over by the barn. I knew I was going to have to do something before it broke in and harmed Trish's chickens, but it soon turned and walked over to a big tree and climbed up into it so quickly I thought it had almost floated up.

That was the last I saw of it, though I stood there for at least another hour until I was so tired I had to give up. I decided to go back to bed and stay awake and watch the monitor, as there was nothing else I could do, but that idea soon gave way to the thought that I wasn't being a very good protector of my family and property, so I stayed up.

I propped a chair next to the window where I could see the tree, made a pot of coffee, then leaned back and drank hot black coffee and watched, the dogs still hiding under the bed, Trish sleeping like a baby. I didn't want to wake her, as there was no point in us both being sleep-deprived the next day.

But of course, as one would expect, the coffee made no difference, and I went to sleep, waking at the crack of dawn.

I jumped up and immediately looked at the monitor, but the

chickens all seemed fine, though they were stirring. I ran back to the window, but I couldn't see if the thing was still in the tree or not.

I was still in my clothes, so I decided to be brave and go see if the thing was still out there. I picked up my shotgun, and the dogs were suddenly by my side, wanting out. I hesitated, then figured the thing must be gone, so I opened the door and we all spilled out into the fresh late-summer air. It was going to be another glorious day.

I walked slowly over to the big tree, the dogs nearby, but saw nothing. I sighed in relief—it was gone. But I quickly noticed a musky odor all around the tree, and when the dogs smelled it, they took off back to the house.

I next went to the barn and let the chickens out. They seemed fine, but I did note that they seemed to stay away from the tree, whereas before they would go over there when it got hotter, enjoying the shade.

I didn't bother to look for tracks. What was the point? Instead, I went inside, the dogs close at my heels, gave them their breakfast, then showered and put on fresh clothes and was soon on my way to the co-op to buy a hotwire, leaving Trish a note. But instead of enough wire to go around the barn, I was going to buy two sets and put one around the tree. I bought two solar chargers and enough wire to fence in whatever I wanted.

Trish had still been asleep when I'd left, but she was up when I returned, making breakfast. It wasn't like her to sleep in so late, and I wondered if she weren't maybe catching a cold or something. I was surprised when she told me she'd had trouble sleeping most of the night, even though she hadn't realized I wasn't in bed. Something had intuitively told her strange things were going on, I guessed, as I told her about what I'd seen.

I spent most of the day setting up the two hotwires, letting the solar chargers get activated, then accidentally testing the one around the barn by forgetting about it and walking right into it. I can say it worked well. These were the types used by horse and cattle ranchers for livestock, not small pet-type chargers, and they packed enough of a punch that they would knock you off your feet if the ground was wet, which I discovered.

Of course, I put the hotwire outside of the pasture fence so the chickens wouldn't get into it. I knew that places like Banff National Park used these same types of hotwires around campgrounds to keep grizzlies out, so I was pretty confident they would keep out our visitor.

I still hesitated to call it a Bigfoot, though I knew in my heart that was exactly what it was. But somehow, by saying the word, I would have to come out of denial, and I didn't really believe these things existed. I told Trish it had been a weird-looking bear, maybe deformed or something.

This was a big mistake, for she immediately began feeling sorry for it and worrying about it, wondering if maybe we shouldn't tell the wildlife people so they would trap it and take it to a vet where it would be cared for. Like I said, she was an animal lover, but she'd grown up in Idaho Falls and wasn't real familiar with wildlife and such. I knew most sickly bears would probably be euthanized, and I told her this, but she was still fretting about it.

What I didn't know was that, in spite of my efforts to scare it away, she started putting out the molasses rolled oats we used for the wild birds in the winter. Molasses oats is pretty tasty to wildlife, and of course it came back.

I didn't know this for some time, as it stayed away from the tree and the barn, and the dogs gradually got to where they were more used to it and even though still nervous, they quit hiding.

Well, as they say, it's not good to feed the wildlife, though I guess birds don't count, as lots of people feed them in the winter, us included. But we found out why you shouldn't feed the wildlife—the hard way, I might add.

I was busy helping my neighbors finish their harvest, mostly just for something to do. They grew Kootenay Specials, a large, burgundy-colored sweet cherry that wasn't ready for harvest until late August.

If I'd been around more, I think I would've noticed the numerous trips Trish was taking to the co-op and the growing stack of bags of molasses oats in the barn. She was feeding the "bear" behind the barn and down the hill a ways, another reason I didn't notice.

Trish is a smart woman and had been a therapist before we both retired, a profession that suited her well, as she's a very compassionate person. She knew better than to feed bears, for Pete's sake, but her empathy got the better of her.

Apparently, it didn't seem to matter how much oats she put out, as it was always gone the next morning. She got to where she would drag an entire 25-pound bag down the hill, and by morning there would be no trace of anything left. On top of that, she would give it all our leftovers, as well as bags of over-ripe fruit she would get from neighbors or road stands.

I guess she figured this so-called bear was getting bigger and stronger and needed all that food. What she expected it to do when fall came, well, I didn't even ask. I guess she thought it would hibernate, but bears hibernate only as a means of surviving winter when there's no food. Bears in captivity typically don't hibernate.

It got to where she was feeding a bag of oats a day, and this was beginning to dig into her retirement check, which she used for incidentals like things the grandkids needed. Of course, with the creature now having its own personal chef, its rampages all up and down the East Shore ended.

It had found a home, even though it seemed to always go down to the lake during the day where it hid somewhere. But at least it left the chickens alone.

Speaking of grandkids, one day Trish decided to go for a week's visit to our daughter's house, which was in a nearby town. I would feed the chickens, but she neglected to tell me about this "bear," which had come to expect a free dinner every night. The upshot was that the creature didn't get fed while she was gone.

She later admitted she was afraid to tell me she'd been feeding it, as she knew better, and also knew I wouldn't be too happy about it. She figured it would be fine on its own for awhile—after all, it was a wild animal.

Trish had been gone a couple of days when I noticed a musty

smell when I went out to feed the chickens and let them out for the day. I knew that smell—it was the same one I'd smelled over by the tree after seeing the Bigfoot for the first time—and the only time, so far, I will add. I knew it was back, and I spent that entire day in trepidation, worrying about the dogs and chickens and whatnot.

That was when I discovered the big stack of bags of oats in the barn, but I figured Trish was just stocking up for the winter, when we fed the quail and pheasants and whatever birds came around.

That evening, after putting the chickens away a bit early, I heard the most terrifying scream I've ever heard in my entire life, and it came from down below the barn. I got my shotgun out, then called the neighbors to see if they'd heard it.

They had and were on high alert, as they had a couple of pet goats. I advised them to get them into some kind of secure shelter, telling them that I'd had this strange creature come up to the house a few weeks before, but since it had left, I hadn't wanted to frighten anyone.

These neighbors were some of those who believed in Flessie, and they wondered if it hadn't come up from the lake. I decided to level with them, telling them what I'd seen. These were the same people I'd been helping with their harvest, so we knew and trusted one another.

Well, they were soon on the grapevine, and I started getting calls. I was actually on the phone with some other neighbors when the scream was repeated, but this time just outside the house. They actually heard it over the phone. By then, the dogs were well under the bed, and it was just me, myself, and I, and all three of us were shaking in our boots.

Except, unbeknownst to me, my neighbors had decided to put an end to all this for once and for all, and were gathering a sort of posse.

I watched out the window, making sure it couldn't see me, and saw it turn and go over to the window where the TV room was and peer inside. Of course, since Trish was gone, the TV was off, so it stood there for a moment, then turned and walked back to the barn.

I had the sinking feeling that it was going to try to get into the barn, but it was getting so dark that, even with the outside lights on, I couldn't tell, so I went into the bedroom where Trish had left the monitor. I knew it had run into the electric hotwire when I heard another scream, this one even angrier than the earlier one.

My phone was ringing, and I answered, watching the monitor, fearing the worst. Another neighbor had called to make sure I was OK, telling me they were coming over. I told them to be careful, as I thought this thing was in the barn, even though I couldn't yet see it on the monitor.

I could now tell the chickens were starting to panic, and I thought of Trish and how much she thought of these birds. There was no way I was going to just sit there and watch them be slaughtered, so I ran outside, shotgun in hand.

Sure enough, the hotwire was down, and it looked like the beast had plowed right through it, for the wires were all twisted and curled together, shorted out. I could also see that the barn door had been literally twisted off its hinges, something even the strongest human could never do.

This gave me pause, for I knew I was about to tangle with something so much more powerful than me that, if the shotgun didn't deter it, I would have no chance.

Now the chickens were half-running, half-flying out the open door, and as they came out, I counted them, making sure all six were there. I was happy to see this, for if the creature came outside after them, I had a much better chance of hitting it with shot, as opposed to trying to deal with it up close inside the barn. Plus I knew the chickens would stand a better chance of getting away.

I expected the thing to come out following, but it didn't. The chickens all disappeared to who knows where, but it was suddenly quiet—deathly quiet—and I suspected this thing was watching, waiting for me to make my move. It had sounded so angry, like it would love to come after whoever had neglected to feed it.

So, there I stood in our dark driveway, watching the barn, dogs hiding under the bed, chickens scattered, when several of my neighbors drove up, all armed with rifles, ready for whatever night terror might be out there, even Flessie, I suspected. They poured from their vehicles like an armed vigilante brigade, loaded for bear, except it was no bear.

It occurred to me that it was all a strange mix of terror and comedy, for the thought of a Bigfoot being in my barn was so ludicrous as to be almost humorous, and the sight of my armed neighbors, so eager to shoot, was more scary than the creature.

I thought of Trish and how she would feel if this thing were killed in cold blood there on our property, and I suddenly felt my fears turn into a sadness. This creature had looked so humanlike, so intelligent, and it had even stood there for the longest time watching television, as if trying to figure it all out. And so far, it hadn't hurt anyone or anything, so why should we kill it?

As my neighbors gathered around, I decided to divert them. I knew it was still in the barn, but I told them I'd seen it go running up the road in the direction of the state park. They excitedly piled back into their vehicles and took off.

Oh great, there was my protection, heading up the road through my own instructions. What was I thinking? This thing was still in the barn, and for all I knew, it would soon come out after me.

I stood there in the dark for the longest time, then decided to go back inside. Maybe I could see something on the monitor.

The monitor was set to give an overview of the area where the chickens were penned, but it had enough of a wide angle that it covered some of the rest of the barn, and I could now see that the door into the storage room was also torn off its hinges. I knew then that it had to be in there, eating oats, of which there were plenty to be eaten.

I decided it was probably safe to go out and try to gather up the chickens. I got my big flashlight and went looking, but I couldn't find even one. I swear, I looked high and low, but they were smart and had hidden somewhere. I found out the next day they were under the front porch, a pretty good place, all in all. They didn't come out until Trish came home, as I called her the next morning and told her all about everything, and she came home early.

I went back into the house after searching for a long time, keeping an eye on the barn as I searched, as I suspected the creature was still inside. I finally coaxed the dogs out from under the bed, making sure they were OK, then watched the monitor.

Surely I would see the Bigfoot when it came back out, as it had to walk through the main part of the barn. There was nothing more I could do, and I was pretty sure at that point the creature would eat its fill and then go back to its hiding place.

I was worried about the chickens, and I finally again went back outside looking for them. It had to be around midnight, and I'd had several calls from my neighbors, asking if I'd seen anything, as they'd come up empty handed.

Things were winding down, as they'd all gone home, but I was sick about the chickens, as I worried a coyote would get them. As I searched, I knew the creature was gone, for I heard the most mournful cry come from far down the hill by the lake.

For a moment I wondered if maybe Flessie weren't real, and that was what I was hearing, but I then knew it was the Bigfoot, for it followed the cry with a scream. I wondered later if it hadn't maybe met Flessie, but had to laugh at myself. The odds were better that it had a massive stomach ache, for when I went into the barn the next morning, I discovered that it had eaten what looked like several bags of oats. I mean, it was a big creature, but not *that* big.

And maybe that was why it never came back. Maybe it associated oats with being sicker than a dog, for there's no way it could've eaten all that and not gotten sick, at least in my opinion.

But it never did come back. Trish came home and found all the chickens, who seemed thirsty and hungry and went right into the barn, where I'd fixed the doors and cleaned up all the spilled oats.

Trish admitted to feeding the creature, which solved the riddle of why it kept coming back, and I really believe it left the area shortly after, as no more reports of it came in. Of course, people still see Flessie, or at least think they do.

I've always laughed at the thought of Flessie, but maybe I shouldn't be so skeptical, for I know most everyone would say the same thing about me seeing a Bigfoot, though there is something a little more personal about seeing a creature in your barn than out in a distant lake. But either way, it's hard to convince people of what you've seen, though I don't try, as nobody would believe me anyway.

But I can tell you one thing for sure—Bigfoot prefers oats to chickens. And I now know why they say you shouldn't feed the wildlife.

8

DON'T HARASS THE WILDLIFE

It had been a great day of catch and release fishing on the Yellowstone River near Livingston, and my group of clients and I were enjoying a nice campfire after a Dutch-oven dinner.

When the inevitable question of what's out there in the dark came up, a guy named Oscar told the following story, which had happened not so far away as the crow flies, on the somewhat nearby Boulder River. —Rusty

Rusty, this happened before drones were so regulated, so I hope no one hangs me for flying my drone in a wilderness area, as there were no rules against it yet. I was a very competent drone pilot at the time, though I switched to radio-controlled aircraft after losing my very expensive craft. Well, OK, I lost a drone, so one may say I wasn't as good of a pilot as I thought, but there were extenuating circumstances, as you'll soon see.

Anyway, a buddy of mine and I lived in Red Cloud, Montana, which is right smack on the edge of the Beartooth Mountains and lots of wilderness. They're beautiful mountains and part of the Greater Yellowstone Ecosystem, and as you well know, there's a lot of wildlife around there.

The event where I lost my drone didn't happen near Red Lodge, though I guess it wasn't too far away as the crow flies. My buddy, Bill, and I did a lot of camping and fishing, though we mostly went for the fishing, the camping only necessary to be close to the fish.

We both had jobs in Red Cloud working maintenance in the lodging business, as Red Cloud's pretty much the gateway to Beartooth Pass, which is famous for sightseeing and also leads to the northeast entrance to Yellowstone. We both hated our jobs and got away every chance we could. We now both live in Helena and have real jobs working out at the airport.

So, we'd heard that the Boulder had some real good fishing, and since we couldn't wait to get away from Red Cloud, we headed over there one Friday evening, since we both had the weekend off, which was rare.

When I say the Boulder, I mean the Boulder River, which flows from the heart of the Beartooths down to the Yellowstone River by Big Timber. It was a bit of a drive for us, but we were anxious to try someplace new, and this fit the bill. We'd heard it was good for brook, brown, cutthroat, and rainbow trout, all pretty good eating.

It's a bit of a drive from Red Cloud to the Boulder, and we got to Boulder Forks pretty late that night, where, just like it sounds, the west and east forks meet the main river. There's a campground there, so we pulled over for the night and slept in the back of my pickup topper instead of pitching our tents.

The next morning, Bill was up fishing before I even stirred. He's much more of a devoted fisherman than I am.

I got up and made us some coffee and hot oatmeal, then joined him on the river for awhile. Like I said, Bill's more of a fisherman than I am, and after not catching anything, I gave up and went and got my drone. When I got bored, I'd take it for a flight, and I have some pretty good videos I've managed to take with it, mostly of the countryside while Bill's fishing.

There wasn't much to see, but I did manage to attract the attention of some guy hanging around, and we got to talking. He told me the fishing was much better on up the road past the ranger station.

Even though it was a bit of a drive, he promised we'd be glad we'd gone on up there.

So, when Bill took a break to come back for more breakfast (he could smell the eggs and bacon I was cooking), I told him what this guy had said, and we were soon heading on up the Boulder, the road narrowing, following what had now become more of a mountain stream than an actual river.

The timber was getting thicker and thicker, and we soon came to the Main Boulder Ranger Station at the head of McLeod Basin under Tepee Mountain. There was nobody at the ranger station or at the nearby campground, where we set up camp. I'd been comfortable enough in my pickup topper so decided to just keep sleeping there, though Bill set up his tent. He said I snored, and he had no desire to engage in another sleepless night.

I remember the mosquitoes being bad enough that we would sit in my truck cab to eat or take breaks, but once near the river, they weren't so bad, as there were enough cool air currents coming off the water to keep them away.

So, Bill went back to fishing, and I sat in my truck, hiding from mosquitoes while trying to decide if I'd rather fish or fly my drone. The drone won, and I was soon flying it up the road, up the creek, and up the side of Tepee Mountain, taking photos and scouting around. I still have a really cool photo I took of Bill from above, on the banks of the Boulder, fly-fishing.

Well, that drone was a people magnet. A couple of guys came from up the road, and when they saw my drone they stopped, wanting to see what I was doing. Remember, this was back when drones were still a novelty.

These two guys were from Livingston, which wasn't all that far away, and I remember one of them being totally enthralled by the drone, saying he was going to get one. I let him fly it a little, and he was hooked, telling me it would be perfect for scouting out wildlife when hunting.

Now, even back then I figured this was illegal, and I told him so, as well as saying that a drone would be more likely to scare off wildlife than help find it. It didn't seem very ethical to me to use a drone for hunting.

I never saw this guy again, but he'd planted a seed. Up until then, I'd thought of my drone only in terms of taking photos of the lay of the land and view from above, but I wondered if it might actually be possible to see wildlife with it. Maybe if you were up high enough so you didn't scare them, you could at least get a feel for what was out there.

I knew we were in grizzly-bear country, and I wondered if I might be able to film a bear or two. The thought intrigued me—to see a bear in its natural habitat without being afraid of it, just watching it for awhile, well, that sounded pretty cool. These days, you'd be arrested for harassing wildlife, and probably with good reason.

Now Bill was back, wanting to move again, as he wasn't catching a thing—he wasn't even seeing any fish jumping. By now it was midafternoon, and I didn't want to pull up camp and go looking for a new place, especially since we had to leave the next day and get back to Red Cloud.

It was a beautiful sunny day, the mosquitoes were gone, but apparently so were the fish. Bill was insistent that we move on, so we pulled up stakes, which didn't take long, and headed farther on up the Boulder. I knew from my Montana map book that something called the Four Mile Guard Station was on up the road, with several campgrounds between it and where we were.

The road became narrow and somewhat windy, tall cliffs on both sides, with small creeks breaking through and merging with the Boulder every so often. My map said they had names like Froze To Death Creek, Speculator Creek, and Weasel Creek. It started feeling wilder and wilder.

Once we reached the Four Mile Guard Station, which was unmanned, we stopped and got out. The road was getting rougher, we didn't know the country, and we had to be home tomorrow night, so I convinced Bill we'd gone far enough. If the fish here refused to bite, well, maybe we should go back to Boulder Forks and just have a nice hotdog dinner and sit around the campfire.

Bill thought I was kidding, but I wasn't. This new place felt closed in and foreboding, and I didn't like it, even though it was beautiful in its own way. It felt like a good place to see a big old grizzly bear—a *hungry* big old grizzly bear.

Bill laughed, got out his rod, and hit the river, though it wasn't much more than a small creek at that point. Like its namesake, it was filled with big slippery boulders with forest coming right down to the edge, and I wondered how Bill was even going to find a good fishing spot. I again got out my drone, though I was rapidly losing interest.

Well, after awhile, Bill had caught not one, but two fish, both rainbows. He said he didn't really like fishing here, as the rocks were too slippery, yet he was beside himself with joy, knowing we'd have a fish fry for dinner, though neither were large enough to make much of a meal. I personally would've tossed them back in, but I didn't say anything. The nearest campground was on up the road a ways, and I was anxious to get settled, so off we went.

It was a pretty enough place with nobody there, though a brown Toyota Tacoma was parked by a sign near a trail that switchbacked up the steep cliffs. We figured someone was backpacking, as my map showed several lakes above.

Bill again pitched his tent while I got a fire going. We'd brought our own wood so didn't have to gather any. I made a big fire, as the mosquitoes were out again in force, knowing the smoke would keep them away until it was dark and we went to bed.

Bill fried up his fish while I cooked some hotdogs on my hotdog poker, then he ate his fish, as well as some of my hotdogs. I didn't mind, as I'd brought plenty, knowing Bill well. He always said he'd catch his own dinner, but he often didn't, so I was prepared.

It was a nice evening, pink alpenglow lingering on the cliffs above, but I felt uneasy, like we were being watched. I finally mentioned this to Bill, wondering if he felt the same, and he finally admitted he did.

We didn't last long around the fire, and Bill headed for his tent while I poured water over the last glowing embers, then climbed into my pickup topper, glad I wasn't in a tent but had instead something a bit more secure.

I guess Bill felt the same way, for sometime during the night he climbed into the back, putting his pad and sleeping bag next to mine.

Knowing he'd awakened me, he whispered, "Did you hear that?"

"Hear what?" I replied.

Now, Bill can be pretty profane when he's really upset, and he just started cussing a blue streak, but still in a whisper. I was mystified. I hadn't heard anything, and yet here was my buddy, obviously scared to death.

I asked him again what he'd heard, but he didn't need to answer, for that was when I heard it also. It came from high above us in the cliffs, yet it was almost as if it was there in the truck with us, as it reverberated like a bass speaker, so low and yet so loud it felt like it cut right through you.

I almost lost it right then and there, fumbling for my keys in the dark, but Bill put his hand over my mouth.

"Don't say anything," he whispered. "It'll hear us. Can you squeeze through the window into the front and get us out of here?"

"No, it's too small," I answered. "I'll have to get out the back and run around."

"Stay inside," he commanded. "Too dangerous."

"What is it?" I asked in a whisper.

"No idea. I have my Magnum, though. We won't go down without a fight."

We lay there in the pitch dark, listening, our hearts beating so loud I was sure whatever it was could hear them, but all was quiet.

I guess we must've fallen asleep, because the next thing I recall seeing was the light hitting the cliffs high above, and I knew it was dawn. Bill was snoring like a sun of a gun, and I knew that was what had awakened me.

I felt much better, no longer as scared, so I quietly opened the topper door and slipped outside, badly needing to relieve myself. That done, I pulled out my camp stove and started making coffee.

Everything seemed perfectly normal, and Bill's tent still stood as it had when he'd pitched it, some 20 feet away. The sound seemed like a bad dream, the sunlight fading it into memory.

Bill was soon up, drinking coffee and making pancakes, but not until he'd gone over and inspected his tent, taking it down. He then wrapped up his gear into a bundle and put it into the back of the truck, and I figured he'd be ready to go after we'd eaten. I knew I was.

We talked a little about the sound in the night, though neither of us said much. Bill told me he thought it was a mountain lion up in the rocks. I didn't argue—he was welcome to think whatever made him feel better about the whole thing.

But then he said he wanted to do a little more fishing. After all, we'd come all the way up here, it was going to be another beautiful Montana day, and he hated to go home without a fish or two for dinner, the rainbows had been so delicious.

I was flabbergasted. How could he even think about fishing after what we'd heard during the night? Did he really think it was a big cat? I knew he didn't, yet I wasn't going to insist we go home without giving him another chance to fish, for I knew I'd never hear the end of it. Besides, it did pretty much seem like a dream at that point, standing there in the bright sunlight.

I looked up at the trail's switchbacks, then decided it might be fun to see what was up there. I'd stay by my truck, messing around with my drone, and let Bill fish. After a couple of hours we'd go on home, and that would be that. The previous night's sound was already fading from my memory.

I took my drone from its case and launched it, flying it back and forth across the canyon, gaining altitude. All the while I was recording with its onboard camera.

I was thinking about that guy from Livingston and what he'd said about seeing wildlife. Maybe, if I could get the drone up above the cliffs, I could eyeball the forest up there and see what was out and about, if anything. I was hoping to maybe see a grizzly and film it. It would definitely be a first for me.

Now the drone was high above, and I tilted it towards the highest cliff and on out over the trees. I knew it had a return to sender option that would make it come back to me if it accidentally flew out of my line of sight, though I'd never tried it out.

The drone hovered above the cliffs, and I could make out myself standing far below. I was feeling cautious, like I might lose it, and was ready to call it back, when I saw something dark standing on a rock looking down into the canyon, and I instantly knew it was watching me!

Now it turned and looked up at the drone—it had to be a grizzly! I couldn't believe it, my first time trying, and I'd found a bear—and not only that, I was filming it. Wait till I showed Bill!

And where exactly was Bill? It had suddenly occurred to me that the bear wasn't that far above us and could possibly reach us very quickly. I scanned the creek behind me, looking for him, but had to pay attention to the drone so I wouldn't crash it.

The drone was still hovering above the bear, but now I could see something else. Someone was coming down the trail! They were still somewhat distant, but I could make out two figures, and they looked like they were carrying backpacks. It had to be the people with the pickup.

Now the bear pulled back into the rocks, still keeping an eye on the drone, but obviously aware that someone was coming. I now felt panicked. I had to somehow make the pair aware there was a bear nearby, a bear that looked like it was now waiting for them!

I didn't know what to do other than to use the drone as a distraction. I swooped it lower and lower, aware that it would soon be out of my sight and control. As it got closer, I could see that I wasn't looking at a bear at all, but something out of my frame of reality. It was now taking turns watching the pair coming down the trail and eyeing the drone, and I could see it was much larger than a bear, stood upright, and had a dark coat with reddish highlights and a very large head, which I was looking directly down upon.

As I lowered the drone a little, it looked up again, and I caught an all too clear view of large eyes, a flat nose, and a face that looked almost like a cross between a human and an ape, yet with its own distinct look.

The pair was still coming, and I was beside myself, not knowing what to do. It was then that the creature screamed, and I recognized the same sound as we'd heard the previous night.

Now Bill was at my side, fishing pole in hand, watching the monitor alongside me, not saying a word. I was glad he was there, for I knew no one would ever believe what I was seeing.

The drone was still hovering, and I could see the creature was getting ready to bat at it. I knew it could easily take it down with one swat. I could see the pair had stopped and were now standing, watching, presumably looking for the source of the scream, yet not able to see the thing because of the rock outcropping.

I suddenly knew what I had to do, and I had to act fast. I backed the drone up, taking it higher into the air above the creature, then I swooped it down as fast as I could make it go, hoping my aim would be good and I wouldn't lose control before it hit.

The last thing I saw before the monitor went dead was a pair of angry, fearful eyes and giant hands reaching upwards for the drone. I thought I'd maybe hit it from the brown color that filled the monitor, though it was possible the creature had caught it.

"Holy hell!" Bill was now swearing over and over again as he threw his gear into the truck and jumped inside, where I quickly joined him.

We sat there, silent, waiting to see if the couple came down the switchbacks, half holding our breath. It seemed like forever before we finally saw two figures running down the trail, packs gone. I watched with fear, wondering if we'd soon see the brown creature close behind, but they were soon down, nothing following.

It was a man and a woman, and the man fumbled in his pockets, then pulled out a set of keys and opened the pickup, and both were soon inside. They started it up and pulled out, passing us, and I could see they were terrified.

We followed them out, but they didn't stop until they got to Big Timber. Once there, they pulled over, and I could see they'd both been crying. I told them we'd seen what had happened, but they didn't want to talk about it, so we exchanged numbers, then all headed our separate ways.

Bill and I didn't talk much on the way home, and I dropped him off at his house in Red Cloud and went on back to my place. I'll never forget the safe and secure feeling I had, doors locked, lights on, neighbors close by in case something happened. I vowed to never live in the country, and I've always wanted to live in town since then, even though before that I'd wanted a cabin out in the woods.

The couple finally called and wanted to come meet with us. They lived in Bozeman, and came over and spent the day, hanging around, talking about what we'd seen, the drone, and how the creature had disappeared into the rocks. They'd waited awhile, then dropped their packs and ran, scared to death.

It had taken them some time to come to grips with it all, and they felt like my drone had saved their lives—well, they didn't actually say my drone, but rather me, but I felt more like I'd simply been a witness at the scene of an accident rather than saving anyone.

To this day, I've never heard a word about my drone, even though it had my ID on it. And if anyone were to find it, I actually wouldn't want it back at this point, as I'd just as soon forget about it all.

Sometimes I think I'd like to have the footage from the camera, then I realize it would just make things worse. What would I do with it? It would be controversial, to say the least, and who wants to open that can of worms?

I have no idea what actually happened—had I injured the thing or merely sidetracked it? I've thought a lot about this, and I think I'm to the point where I hope it's dead, though I suspect it destroyed my drone, or someone would've found it.

It was just too sinister looking and sounding, and I don't think it had anyone's well-being in mind, though maybe it was just bluffing. I'll never know, which is just how it is, and I've come to accept that.

But later, Rusty, after reading your stories from Yellowstone, I wondered if this thing wasn't related to what's been going on down there, as we weren't that far away, maybe only about 20 miles.

But what was really strange was when I was studying the area later, looking through my maps, I found we were only a few miles from a place called Baboon Mountain. Where in heck would a name like that come from?

I'm glad it's over, but I will say it's the only time in my life I've harassed the wildlife—but it had it coming.

9

OLD HOLLOWTOP

As I've mentioned before, even though I live in Colorado, I sometimes go to Montana to help my friend out when he gets busy, partly because I love Montana fishing.

Peter and I hooked up when he called my fly-fishing buddy in Bozeman, wanting someone to come and give a demonstration to some middle-school kids. I volunteered to go, and it turned out to be a lot of fun. Peter first showed a really nice film about fly-fishing, then we all went to a local stream and practiced. I found out later that Peter had made the film, as he had a degree in filmmaking.

We went out for lunch after getting the kids all back to their school, and we got to talking, one thing leading to another, as things often tend to do.
—Rusty

I have a degree in nature filmmaking, and though I don't work for National Geographic or any of those big guns, I do have footage that I'm sure they'd pay big bucks to have. Ironically, they'll never see it, even though they helped pay for my degree—well, not NatGeo, but rather, the Discovery Channel.

Let me explain. I got my degree, a Master's of Fine Arts in Nature

Filmmaking, from a Montana university, and that degree was part of a program subsidized by the Discovery Channel.

It's a very exclusive and hard to get into, only accepting about a dozen students a year and taking two to three years to complete. But in all honesty, one can teach themselves pretty much what I paid a fortune to learn.

Filmmaking isn't like engineering or medicine, it's pretty straightforward. Sure, you got to practice on expensive equipment at the university that you wouldn't have access to otherwise, but the way things are going, you don't need that kind of equipment to make films anymore anyway.

Part of the requirement to graduate was to make a film of a certain length and quality. It was kind of like writing a thesis would be in most graduate programs. You had to pick a topic and coordinate with your advisor and all that, then you'd spend a lot of time making the film.

After you finished all the required classes, you were free to leave and go wherever you wanted, make your film, then come back to defend it, which basically just meant showing it to your committee and answering their questions.

Most of the students stayed close to the university because they couldn't afford their own equipment, but I had my own camera, an older Canon, and I also had a nice Mac setup with Final Cut Pro for editing. This meant I could go wherever I wanted.

I'd made a few good friends in my cohort, as we had common interests—nature and film, and most everyone seemed to focus more on birds and wildlife for their films, as well as on Yellowstone and Glacier national parks, and there was one guy who was doing something about the geology of Bighorn Lake over in central Montana. This all made sense, since it's a nature film program, but I wanted to do something different.

I decided to do something about the Tobacco Root Mountains, which is a small range west of Bozeman. For some reason, I was fascinated by the area, and I think part of it had to do with the town of Pony, which I'd been to several times and really liked.

I talked with my advisor, and we came up with a working thesis—
I would film sunrise and sunset from the tops of as many peaks as I
could climb in an attempt to really show the grandeur of the place. In
addition, I would do some night shots of the Milky Way and constel-
lations from up high.

It would be a lot more ambitious than just doing something about
say, moose or bears, but it would also be much more original. It was
my chance to do something really unique, and I had visions of it cata-
pulting me to a job with one of the big guns, like NatGeo.

So, I was going to climb and film as many peaks as I could—
Montana scenery from the rooftops, or maybe I should say the *Root*-
tops, as the Tobacco Roots are called the *Roots* by the locals.

I knew some were very difficult to climb, and I was no technical
climber, but I also knew some were easy walkups, as long as you
didn't mind a little altitude gain. With 43 peaks higher than 10,000
feet, there was no way I could climb them all, so I would just pick the
easiest ones.

This sounded very freeing after having to study film theory and
whatnot, let me tell you. The highest peak is Hollowtop, at 10,604
feet, a prominent caved-in looking mountain one could see for miles,
and that was where I wanted to start the project.

I would have to get used to the idea of either spending the night
on top of the peaks or climbing in the dark or maybe both, plus I'd
have to get some good equipment, a strong headlamp being one—
or maybe two in case one failed. And I needed to get in better
shape.

I was living in Bozeman, which isn't far from the Roots, so it didn't
seem like the logistics would be too difficult, at least in terms of
getting there. But the first thing I needed to do was research the area
and figure out where the best places to spend my time would be. I
was nearing the end of my second year, and I'd have all summer to
explore and film.

I'll never forget the evening I started my research. I started by
keying in, for some strange reason, the words *Old Hollowtop* instead of
just *Hollowtop*. I don't know where I got the idea it was called *Old*

Hollowtop, maybe I'd heard someone call it that, but the results of that search were very strange.

Instead of taking me to Hollowtop Mountain, I found myself looking at a strange and very fuzzy photo of what looked to be a combination of an ape and a bald eagle with a humanoid face. I say a bald eagle because this ape-like thing was all black but had a yellow-white head with what looked like yellow-white feathers coming down around its neck, just like an eagle has.

It was a creature called Old Yellowtop, which had been sighted various times in some area of Ontario over a period of over 65 years, and what looked to be feathers was actually thick cloak-like hair. It had been seen by a number of people, and some felt it was a relative of the Sasquatch, or Bigfoot, maybe one with odd coloring.

OK, I'm a naturalist, not a cryptologist, and I actually didn't even know there was a field called cryptology until then. I had a good laugh, then went back to reading about Hollowtop Mountain.

But this thing had captured my attention, and it carried with it a sense of intrigue. Was it a hoax, or had people actually seen it? The few sightings seemed authentic, as they were quite a bit apart in time, and it was long ago, back in the early 1900s, before the topic of Bigfoot became popular.

I did a search on Bigfoot and Tobacco Root and found nothing, but the search did lead me to other accounts of sightings in Montana that were much more recent—food for thought, but I still figured it was all a big hoax.

People love to trick one another, it's part of human nature, and what better than to see some big hairy ape out in the wilds—supposedly, anyway—and scare your buddies half silly? Great fun, if you were into jokes and being a trickster, which I wasn't.

But back to my film. I needed to finish it by the end of summer so I could defend it in the fall and avoid having to pay more tuition. It typically takes longer to edit a film than to actually film it, unless you're a real pro, which I wasn't, so I knew time was of the essence. If I could get up into the mountains and get all my footage by late-summer, I might be able to pull it off. The problem was, the mountains weren't usually accessible until early July because of the snow, sometimes later, and the summits were going to be even more inaccessible.

I'd read that Hollowtop was one of the easier peaks to get to from the east side of the range, which would save me lots of driving time, as Bozeman was closer to the east side than the west. It could be accessed by a trail from the small town of Pony that led to Hollowtop Lake, which sat in the cusp of the mountain.

I could basecamp there at the lake, climbing the peak and spending the night on top. The most critical factor in all this was choosing days with good weather forecasts, which could be tricky with summer rains.

Pony is an old gold-mining town at the base of the mountain with maybe 100 people, if that, but it once had 5,000. The Roots are not as pristine as one might think, but were once the site of numerous gold mines and prospect claims that date from the 1880s, which resulted in a lot of access roads. They're only about 26 miles from north to south and 18 miles wide, so we're not talking about a really big range here, and I think this is why I was so surprised with what I found there. I would expect it in a big wilderness area like Yellowstone or Glacier. But more on that later.

Well, I worked hard all through the early part of the summer, researching and making the parts of my film that I could, things like the introduction and rough script. I kept track of the snows by calling a fellow in Pony I'd met earlier at a Ken Burns documentary in Bozeman, which actually gave me some good ideas.

This guy, who I'll call Ben, lived in Pony and kept me up to date on how much snow there was on Hollowtop, at least as far as he could tell. He was very enthused about my project and wanted to be of help, and being retired, he had lots of time. We actually ended up spending hours on the phone, and he ended up being more help than my advisor with tons of good ideas.

One morning, along in mid-July, Ben called. I'd been fretting about getting started on the filming part of my project, worried that it wouldn't be until mid- to late-August before I'd be able to get up there.

I was relieved when he said he'd run into a couple of climbers who had just done not only Hollowtop, but the mountain next to it, Jefferson, which was the third highest in the range at 10,513. They'd said there were still a couple of big cornices and some snowbanks, but if one were careful, they could be negotiated. They'd actually done both in one day, coming up from North Willow Creek Trail, which started just outside of Pony.

Ben went on to say that they'd had to do some bushwhacking and scrambling, but the views were tremendous. He'd told them about my project, and they said it would be a very cold night on either mountain and to dress warm. He said they'd also mentioned something else, then he hesitated and told me to never mind, it wasn't important.

I was, of course, now curious, but he insisted it wasn't anything relevant, and he'd tell me in person. I let it go, but later wished I hadn't, as it might have saved me a lot of grief had I known, though *grief* really isn't a strong enough word—pain and suffering might fit better.

I'd managed to get all the equipment I needed, which included a super warm down bag, a small backpacking bivy sack, spikes for my heavy-duty boots, headlamps, a GPS, and lots of freeze-dried food and a small stove. On top of that, I had a super lightweight carbon-fiber tripod, my somewhat heavy film camera, extra batteries, and everything I needed to shoot. All in all, even though everything was as lightweight as I could get, I was still carrying a 60-pound pack.

I knew I'd have to leave most of it at Hollowtop Lake and base-camp from there, but I stood a good chance of summiting not one, but two peaks, and it would be a good start to getting this project going. I could go back to Bozeman and see how the film turned out, then plot the next few peaks. Maybe I could even actually finish before fall.

And I will admit that, at this point, the thought of doing a coffee-table book of still shots was now front and center. I could already see some of the photos—the outlines of the high mountains against a full-on panorama of the Milky Way, stars blazing in blues and yellows and whites.

Well, wagons ho! What a disappointment I was in for, though I had no idea at that point, fueled by ambition and excitement and who knows what else?

I was soon on the trail to Hollowtop Lake, a good 10 miles from Pony, following along Willow Creek in the shade of the Deer Lodge National Forest. Ben had said that the hike was fairly popular, but I didn't see anyone else, except for Ben, of course, who was accompanying me to the lake, helping me carry my gear in. I think he was as excited as I was.

It took us about six hours to reach the lake, and I was happy to see it, for my shoulders were starting to ache from the heavy pack. I was glad I wouldn't be trying to climb with it.

The lake was really nice, and after I set up my bivy sack, Ben and I had a nice afternoon snack there on the shore, watching the trout jump. He didn't stay long, as he wanted to get back down to Pony before dark. Actually, he acted kind of nervous and kept looking around to the point that I actually asked him about it.

He hesitated, but finally told me the rest of the story he'd gotten from the climbers. He said they'd climbed up the southern face of Jefferson, which was mostly across loose scree, though about halfway up it became more stable. They couldn't see anyone, but they kept hearing rockfall behind them, as if someone was climbing just out of their sight.

At first, they didn't think much of it, figuring it was just another climbing party, but when they would stop, it would, too, and they finally started feeling uneasy. After reaching the top of Jefferson, they could see Hollowtop to the north, and knowing it was a relatively easy hike to its summit, they decided to go for it.

There's a couloir between the two peaks, and they glissaded down this, then began hiking towards some small alpine lakes, finally working their way through thick forest with lots of large rocks and boulders. This was when they started hearing a strange barking sound behind them.

Well, they knew there were wolves in the area, so they proceeded, thinking that's what it probably was. They finally made it to the top of Hollowtop, but were losing the light at that point, so they came down as fast as they could, once again feeling as if they were being followed.

At this point, they'd planned on sleeping by the lake in their hammocks, but decided instead to hike on out in the dark, even though they were exhausted. They made it down to Pony well after midnight, where they camped behind one of the old buildings there, then met Ben the next morning as he was out walking his dog. He'd given them a ride back to their car, and they'd told him this story.

Ben now told me he had decided not to say anything lest I cancel my long-laid plans. There really wasn't much to the story, he said, just some barking noises and the feeling of being followed—probably coyotes, as he'd heard them make the same sound.

We talked for awhile, and he even offered to help me carry my stuff back down to Pony, should I decide to not stay. But it was still daylight, and things felt fine, and there was no way I was going to cancel my plans. I'd have to start over, and then what? I risked not finishing my degree over some vague night sounds, which was craziness.

Would I have proceeded with my plans even if Ben had told me all this when we were back in town? Yes, and I told Ben this, reassuring him things would be fine. I had plenty of bear spray, two cans actually, and nothing would bother me.

That night was calm and peaceful, and I set up my camera and got some beautiful night shots of the stars over Hollowtop Lake. A couple of fishermen had come in and were camped a bit down the lakeshore from me, and I got one photo of their campfire under the stars that was very evocative.

Hollowtop Mountain was visible in the background above the lake, as there was enough starshine that the mountain was lit up if I set my camera on a long exposure.

It was so quiet and peaceful, and I fell asleep with nary a care, happy to be there. I would sleep in the next morning, taking it easy, then gear up for the climb up Hollowtop that afternoon and spend the night there. I was kind of nervous, yet excited. Camping on the top of a 10,000-foot mountain was going to be an experience I'd never forget. And it turned out to be exactly that, but not in the way I'd expected.

I woke late, the sun filtering through the trees into my bivy sack, mosquitoes hitting against the mesh top, trying to get in for a breakfast meal. I lay there for a long time, waiting for the sun to make them retreat, but it was soon too hot inside and I got up.

I hate Deet, but sprayed some on, which made the skeeters tolerable enough that I could make breakfast. I then went down by the lakeshore and sat on a big log, contemplating the day ahead, drinking a cup of tea.

The skeeters had followed me there, and I was finally so frustrated that I decided to just head on up Hollowtop, where I knew they wouldn't bother me.

I got out my pack and started packing it with what I thought I would need—down coat, sleeping bag, warm socks, spikes, etc. It seemed like I was taking everything, so I stopped, emptied my pack, and started over, taking only the bare essentials and leaving the rest in a stuff sack behind a tree. I didn't need any extra weight, as my camera gear was heavy enough.

I was soon climbing, though very slowly, but that was OK, as I had plenty of time to get to the top, and going slow would help me acclimate. I stopped every so often to take photos and to film birds and such, and I think I set a record for the slowest ascent of the mountain ever, getting there just as the sun was getting ready to set.

I quickly set up my camera and recorded one of the most fantastic sunsets I've ever seen, pink and gold clouds to the west and alpenglow slowly melting down the numerous mountains all around me like honey, especially nearby Mount Jefferson.

Oh man, was I stoked! And I knew it was just the beginning, as the night sky was going to be unbelievable, the clouds slowly moving away to the north. It was going to be a perfectly clear night.

It then dawned on me that it was going to be pretty dark up there, and I would be wise to take a look around and get my bearings, picking out a place to sleep where I wouldn't be in danger of rolling off.

I found a place between two large rocks that felt pretty secure, and I laid out my sleeping bag and night gear. I ate a dinner of granola bars and cheese, drank some water, then waited for the night sky to open, all the while watching the peaks all around me and filming as the pink glow of the Belt of Venus faded and the shadows descended.

It was soon cold—bone-chilling cold—and I put on my wool longjohns and socks, wool pants, and wool sweater. I also had those hand warmer packages you can put in your boots and gloves, but I wanted to save them for later when I knew it would be brutally cold.

I kicked back against a rock and waited for the stars to show their faces, watching several jets floating through the sky far away, lights blinking, maybe even heading for the Bozeman airport some 50 miles distant. I wondered who was on them and if they had any inkling there was a lone human watching from the top of a 10,000-foot peak far below.

I can't begin to describe how primal it felt up there, all alone in a sea of stars and mountains, no one around, and no lights visible anywhere to even remind me that there were other humans on the planet, the jets now gone. I began to feel like I was the last survivor of a doomed race, insignificant, lost, and alone. I was actually starting to panic a bit when I realized what was going on—I was feeling the lack of oxygen! I had to take deep breaths and try to increase my intake, or I would soon become hypoxic, a condition that affected climbers, leading to irrational decisions.

It was getting colder by the minute, so I wrapped my camera under my coat next to me to keep the batteries from getting too cold. I then sat back, taking deep breaths, then promptly went to sleep, though I hadn't intended to. The lack of oxygen and stiff climb had gotten to me.

When I woke, it took a minute to remember where I was, sitting there under the most magnificent night sky, the Milky Way spilling across like a three-dimensional sash of deep blue studded with the purist whitest diamonds imaginable, a red one shining here and there.

It took my breath away, and I was soon filming it, knowing I was experiencing one of the highlights of my new film career, of my entire life.

But what the heck! Clouds were moving in! It was predicted to be good weather, but the sky was rapidly filling with black clouds, blocking my view.

I pulled back from the camera, only to see that what I'd thought were clouds was moving around. There was someone else up here!

I instinctively crouched down into the rocks, not wanting to be seen. What were other people doing up here? I hadn't heard anyone coming, but then, I'd been asleep.

I then recalled reading about the Hayden Survey, the group who had climbed and mapped many of the West's mountains in the 1800s, and how they'd seen a grizzly on top of one big peak, though I couldn't recall where, and I wondered if a bear hadn't come up Hollowtop. It wasn't a difficult climb, and a bear could easily climb it. If I didn't panic, maybe I could get some very unusual shots of it in profile against the stars.

I quietly turned my camera back on, then reached into my pack for my bear spray. Whatever it was, I knew it would be just as surprised to see me up here as I was it, but hopefully it would just go back down and never see me. In the meantime, maybe I could get something that would make my film much more interesting, to say the least.

But now I could see that there were two of them! Did grizzlies hang together like that? I didn't think so. Everything I'd ever read about them said they were solitary animals, unless they were mating or had cubs.

I shivered, taking the safety off my can of spray, being totally quiet, breathing as softly as possible, all the while my camera going. My mind was also going, as I wondered if it could possibly be people —maybe someone else had climbed during the night to take sunrise photos. Should I say something? My instincts said not to.

From nowhere, I flashed back on Old Yellowtop and all the reading I'd done. A chill went through me. Were these Bigfoot? They certainly seemed to have the bulk and height, and that would account for there being two of them.

Now a throaty call came through the night from far away, sounding like maybe over from the top of Jefferson. The two figures stood still, then one called back.

It was a loud mournful sound, and I can't really compare it to anything, but it left my blood colder than it already was. I knew then I wasn't dealing with anything even vaguely human.

I desperately needed to get my foot and hand warmers, as my extremities were now going numb, but I was afraid to hardly breathe, yet alone move. And it was right then that a stench wafted through the air, apparently coming from the creatures, and I coughed involuntarily, silently cursing myself.

The creature nearest me turned as if listening, then it quickly came towards me. I was terrified, holding the can of bear spray up, even though all I could see was a dark shadow. But when the shadow took on form and I could make out large yellow eyes and teeth in the starlight, I pulled the trigger, hitting the creature right between the eyes with the bear spray, which is basically hot capsaicin pepper.

The creature reared back as if not knowing what had hit it, then began flailing around, trying to clear its eyes with its giant hands. The other creature was now right by me, and I let go with the second half of the can, also hitting it, but not before it had lobbed what had to have been a rock straight at me.

I recall something large flying by my head, one corner of it glancing off my jaw, and the impact knocked me backwards from where I'd been crouched down.

As I lay there reeling, I heard what sounded like a cry of terror, and it seemed to me that one of the creatures was falling from the mountaintop, as the cry became more and more faint.

The other creature also appeared to be gone, and I wondered if it hadn't gone after the other. I soon heard a call come from what seemed to be a ways down the mountainside.

I could now taste blood, and the entire side of my head felt numb. I knew I was injured, but I had no idea how severely. All I could think of was that I had to get back down off the mountain to the lake before these things came back looking for me. If one had indeed fallen off the mountain, there was no doubt it was dead or severely injured, and the others would be likely to want revenge.

I don't recall much after that, except grabbing my camera and stuffing it into my pack, getting my headlamp and the other can of bear spray, and trying to remember the path I'd taken up the mountain.

Oh, and I do remember knowing I was injured and would be going into shock before long and had little time to get down to the lake where maybe the fishermen still were, a task that seemed impossible.

Down, down, down I went in the starlight, and I recall thinking I would be better off not turning on my headlamp unless I absolutely had to, as it would tell the creatures my location. I'd been sitting in the dark for hours, and my night vision was better than I'd expected.

It didn't take long before the numbness wore off and I started to feel the pain. I kept having to spit out blood, and I knew I had to stop the bleeding somehow, so I stopped long enough to rip a piece off my longjohn top and stuff it inside my mouth, biting down, though something didn't seem to work right.

The night seemed endless, and I did have to finally turn on my headlamp when I got back down into the forest. I had somehow miraculously made my way back to the lake, where I collapsed.

When I woke, I was in agony, my jaw feeling like it was broken, blood still seeping out of the compress I'd made. I ripped off another piece and stuffed it in my mouth, then tried to stand and get my bearings. I was weak and felt like I was going to die, but I knew I had to keep going.

I somehow found the trail back to Pony, but I didn't get very far. The next thing I knew, I was in an emergency room in Bozeman, having been found by some hikers and airlifted out by chopper. I'd lost a lot of blood and several teeth and my jaw was broken, but I would live, in spite of the pain.

All I could think of was my camera, even while I was told I would be undergoing emergency surgery. Believe it or not, I didn't care about having a film of the creatures, but I badly wanted that sunset and the photos I'd taken of the Milky Way. It had been a once in a lifetime thing for me, as I knew I would never go back up on a peak like that, at least not in the dark.

I had to have several sessions with an oral surgeon that involved bone grafts to my jaw, then later, when that had healed, some dental implants, but I will say I recovered with no long-term impacts, other than my insurance co-pay. Since I'd been a student when it happened, I was insured through the university, which was a very good thing.

The pain had been significant, but after awhile I decided I didn't want to take any more painkillers, so I just focused on my film when things would start to hurt. I finally healed up after a few months to where I was pain free, though the grafts took much longer.

And what about my camera? Well, I did get it back eventually, as the hikers who'd found it had carried it out, and someone else had even found my pack and stuff behind the bush before the snows hit. Since Ben knew what had happened, he was able to get it all to me, which I was very grateful for.

And Ben was there with me when I finally decided it was time to see what the memory card held. He'd offered for me to recuperate at his house there in Pony, and he and his wife were the main reason I'd done so well, as they took very good care of me.

Just as I'd hoped, the sunset and night-sky shots were absolutely world-class, and I did end up using them in my thesis film, though it would be a couple of semesters later, as the university granted me a leave of absence until I healed up. But the Bigfoot shots? Well, I never showed them to Ben and his wife. I knew they would be scared to death, living so close.

But when I looked at that part of the film, both creatures were there, at first just vague dark outlines against the stars, but then, when the first creature came for me, there was a terrifying mix of teeth and large eyes and blackness, a true nightmare.

I watched that film over and over in disbelief, and I guess I must have hoped it had all been a dream until then. The pictures didn't lie, and I swore to never show the film to anyone.

Why? I really don't know, but I did come up with a theory later. It seemed that these beings, these things called Bigfoot, just like the grizzly bear, had been pushed into wilder and wilder habitat by us humans, most of who refused to even acknowledge their existence. Were they now having to hide on the tops of high peaks for safety and solace? And even that didn't seem to be good enough, with climbers and people like me around.

Had the Bigfoot actually fallen off the cliffs after I'd sprayed it? I felt somewhat bad thinking this, as I knew they were probably sick and tired of people everywhere, and yet, they seemed to be following others and had tried to kill me, so why would I feel sorry?

I don't know, but I do know that after that, I changed my film thesis to fly-fishing in Montana's many rivers. I got my degree and now teach outdoor education, trying to introduce kids to the great outdoors, and I must say I really enjoy it.

I never talk much about what happened, other than to say I fell and hit my jaw, and people seem satisfied with that explanation. In some ways, I would like people to know, but in the long run, it doesn't seem worth it. I've read some of the comments about people who've had sightings and they're generally not very kind. And as an educator, I feel like I need to be careful about my reputation, as I'm teaching and caring for people's kids, so I just let it be.

I do still go out in the mountains sometimes, but as long as I stay away from the Roots, I figure all is OK.

10

THE FIDDLER ON THE DECK

I met Orin when guiding a fishing trip in my home state of Colorado. He'd been given the trip for his 50th birthday as a gift from his wife and kids, and he sure seemed to be enjoying himself. He and his wife owned a small ranch not too far away, where they raised alpacas in the shadow of magnificent Mt. Sopris, selling the wool to weavers.

We were fishing the Frying Pan River, one of the state's premier trout fisheries, when we heard a noise in the thick brush along the creek. I laughed when Orin said it was maybe a Bigfoot.

It turned out to be a deer, but I later asked him if he believed in Bigfoot. He said he did and later told the following story over one of my traditional Dutch-oven dinners, a story that I found to be both moving and poignant. It gave me real insight into the kind of guy he was, and he's someone I now value as a friend. —Rusty

R usty, my name's Orin and I come from a long line of musicians. My grandfather played cello with the Boston Philharmonic, and my grandmother played harp for private events, you know, like weddings and such, all in Boston. Their daughter, my mom, played piano and later harp, then moved to Montana for college, of all places, where she met my dad.

My dad's side was also musical, but they came from the Missouri Ozarks and had their own ideas about the subject. My dad played dobro and guitar. I'm always amazed when I think of how different my mom and dad were, but they say opposites attract.

In any case, I grew up in the middle of all this, in rural Montana, listening to my mom play classical piano and harp and my dad play bluegrass dobro and country guitar—oh, and he also played a mean harmonica.

My older sister took lessons from my mom and became a pretty good pianist herself, sometimes playing for school events, church, that kind of thing, but never professionally. I grew up refusing to play anything, always the rebel, though I did once threaten to take up bagpipes when my mom wouldn't leave me alone about taking lessons.

But I always liked music, as long as it wasn't classical or bluegrass —or folk, I hated folk. So what did that leave? Rock and roll, baby. But the closest I ever got to playing rock and roll was on my stereo.

If they had an award for disappointing your parents, I'd be first in line. I not only refused to play an instrument, I also refused to go to college. My dad didn't really care, as he'd dropped out of college and was a lineman, but it basically killed my mom, for she had a university education, as did her entire family. Like I said, how those two ever got together is a mystery.

Instead of being a doctor or such like my mom wanted, I became a finish carpenter. I love working with wood, and there are lots of nice houses near Kalispell with beautiful custom cabinets and such that have my signature on them—well, not literally, but my work really stands out. I hope I don't sound like a braggart, but I guess I still feel a little insecure about not being a professional with a college degree— thanks to my mom, though I love her dearly. Oh, and my sis became a dentist, so I should thank her, too, I guess.

But I was the one who got to live on the edge of some of the most beautiful wild country in the United States, maybe all of North America, because I built my own house on 80 acres I'd bought back before things got so expensive.

Where was it? Right on the boundary of Glacier National Park near West Glacier, Montana. I got to live in a landscape that a lot of people only dream of. My wife and I had a house that wasn't just beautiful inside, but beautiful in every direction you looked. It was like living in a landscape painting. My sis lives in a fancy subdivision in Denver, with her neighbor's fence for a view.

Living close to nature is good for you. When I die, I want my obit to read something like, "He always lived in the most beautiful places," just like the one for the famous artist Russell Chatham read. Chatham also lived in Montana.

Well, they say you always eventually go home, and when you get older, I think it's true, you go back to what you grew up with. And for me, that was music.

I was in my early 40s, and I'd finally got to the place where I could afford to take some time off now and then. My wife, Becky, worked in the billing office of a medical clinic, and her income gave us some stability, so I didn't worry when I was between jobs.

Actually, my work was more and more in demand as wealthy people discovered the area, and I was keeping really busy. I'd just finished a big job, an expensive house owned by a celebrity singer down in Lakeside, and I needed a break.

So, I took a month off and just kicked back, taking it easy, working on some projects around the house, cooking a lot—I love to cook— cleaning and doing the laundry, and taking care of our two kids, though being in high school, neither required much care. Becky got to where she hoped I wouldn't go back to work, as she now had a house-husband, but after a week I started getting bored.

One day I'd gone to downtown Kalispell for something or other, and I happened to notice a pawn shop. I'm all for a bargain, so I went inside, and there, lo and behold, was a violin!

I stood there, dumbfounded, as a whole host of feelings came from nowhere, feelings of nostalgia and of visiting my grandparents in their big old Boston house when I was a kid, them serenading us on the cello and harp.

I didn't even think about it, I just bought the darn thing and walked out the door, no idea what I was going to do with it.

Well, what I did with it was become obsessed. I guess all those musical genes raised their ugly heads, because all I wanted to do was learn to play that darn violin. I couldn't read a lick of music, so I took it up by ear, and I will say I seemed to have a bit of talent for it, as it came pretty easily, and I knew violin wasn't an easy instrument to learn.

But I didn't want to learn to play violin, I wanted to learn to play the fiddle. For all practical purposes, they're the same instrument, the terms just referring to how you play it—violin is classical, while fiddle is bluegrass.

Growing up in rural Montana, you don't hear much classical music, and there can be a bit of a highbrow association with it. And even though I seemed to be going back to my musical roots, I had no intention of playing classical, as I hadn't lost my mind, not yet, anyway. It was too hard and too stuffy and formal for my tastes.

I just wanted to play fiddle. I'd apparently lost my dislike of bluegrass. I bought a couple of books, but I don't remember even reading them, I just practiced and practiced.

Well, as far as Becky was concerned, I might've just started drinking, though fiddle playing was a lot more intrusive. I'm not saying she wasn't supportive, as she was, but she was much more supportive when I didn't practice where she could hear me. So, I played in the basement, spending every spare minute practicing. Maybe I would've been better off drinking—it's not as noisy.

Well, my wife was probably wondering what next, but she had no idea. I started getting interested in venues where people played fiddle. I say venues, but I didn't care whether it was something like the Red Ants Pants Music Festival over by White Sulphur Springs or an open mic at the local bar. I just wanted to hear other people play the fiddle and see how they did it. It was like learning a foreign language—full immersion is the best.

I started going out a lot. I think Becky at first thought I was having a mid-life crises, and maybe I was, but it wasn't your usual kind. I'd sometimes take the kids with me, or sometimes Becky would go, or I'd go alone, I didn't care.

I'd talk to the musicians and see how they did things. Becky said I should get a job covering the music beat for the paper, and I was so nuts I actually considered it for a minute, even though I'm not much of a writer.

I finally got a job doing cabinets in a new house over in Columbia Falls, but even on my breaks I'd play that darn fiddle. I was actually getting to where I could play some tunes pretty good, or at least that's what my daughter Kim told me.

Well, one evening after work I got tired of the basement and took my fiddle out onto the back deck. Like I said, we had 80 acres, and it was mostly thick timber, but you could see the tall mountains of Glacier in the distance.

While out there playing, I felt different. I realized I felt free and unfettered, and after that, I'd play out on the deck as long as the weather allowed, even at night.

You can probably see where this is going. Playing out in nature, I was sure to become a curiosity for whatever was around, and that's exactly what happened. Animals are smart, and it behooves them to know what's in their environment. They're naturally curious.

I found that, if I played during the day, the squirrels and birds would come around as if to listen. In the evening, it would be the deer and an occasional fox or coyote. But I wasn't really prepared for what eventually came around.

I like Irish music, and I was getting to where I could play some jigs and reels and that kind of thing. Irish music is hard to play, so I must have been getting better. A lot of bluegrass has its origins in Irish and Scottish music.

Part of what I liked about it was that it was so lively and fun. So, I'd be out there on our back deck stomping around and playing some enthusiastic bluegrass, all caught up in it, and then look up to see I had an audience—a couple of deer, maybe a few bluejays, a rabbit, that kind of thing, though usually not at the same time.

If the weather was nice, I'd sometimes do a barbecue for dinner and Becky and the kids would come out and listen to me play while eating. I would play quieter music then so as to not run them off, stuff like ballads, that same folk music I'd always hated.

By then, Becky was starting to appreciate my efforts more, and she'd sit and listen, saying it was all so lovely, music out in the woods. This made me feel really good, and I started to get an inkling of why my mom's family had loved music so much.

Well, barbecue and bluegrass, what could go better together? Apparently, we weren't the only ones who liked that combination. I think it was the smell of the barbecue that first brought my new audience to me, but I do think the music helped keep them around.

But I'm getting ahead of myself.

One evening, I'd pretty much played myself out, and it was getting late. I was sitting in one of the deck chairs, and my daughter Kim came out and joined me. We talked about school and her future plans and life in general, and she finally told me, "Dad, you're getting pretty good on that thing. I really admire your ability to focus and stick with something so hard."

I was pleased to hear it, telling her that maybe someday I'd be good enough to play in front of a real audience, like at the Red Ants Pants. She'd gone with me not long before, and we'd both really enjoyed it.

I was surprised by her reply.

"Don't do it, Dad. The pressure just ruins it. That's why I quit drama. I love acting, but having an audience changes everything. It's no longer fun."

I knew she'd quit her high-school drama class, but I hadn't known why until then.

"Some people love an audience," I replied. "It motivates them to do even better, and creates a kind of synergy."

"I know," she replied. "But Dad, I know you too well. You're not going to like it. Like you always tell us, know thyself."

Ah, the wisdom of children. I wish I'd listened, but instead, a seed had been planted. I wanted to join a group. Maybe I actually was reliving my younger days, or at least I knew Becky thought so.

Before I knew it, I'd managed to hook up with several other guys who had the same idea. We said our main goal was to have fun, but I knew that in the back of all of our minds we wanted to play semi-professionally, or at least in front of a real audience. And, of course, since I lived out in the woods, it made sense for us to practice on our back deck.

And man, did we have fun. We had one guy on the guitar, one on harmonica, one on steel guitar, and me on fiddle. Our guitar player also sang, and I did backup vocals, discovering that I had a pretty nice tenor voice, or at least that's what the guys told me. We'd do a potluck barbecue on Friday evenings after work, then play until we could play no more. It got to where their spouses, friends, kids, you name it would come along, and it eventually turned into one big party, every Friday night.

Well, one summer night, everyone had gone home except Wes, my buddy who played guitar, and we were sitting around in the dark, winding down and talking.

Wes was feeling like we'd reached a dead end with the band, and he wanted to branch out. I was surprised, thinking we were just getting going good, but he wanted to start playing more Western tunes. He wanted me to sing more lead, as he felt I had a good voice and it would add variety. He said I should learn to yodel.

I got a good laugh from this, I can tell you, and as we sat there talking, I felt a sense of nostalgia come over me, a farawayness, like I was suddenly a part of something bigger than me.

I looked out at the dark forest all around us, only half listening to Wes talk about some guy he'd met called Wiley who had a band called Wiley and the Wild West. They sang authentic old tunes like *Cattle Call* and *Red River Valley*. Wiley was apparently a rancher out by the Highline in the central part of the state, called that because it was the northern route of the Burlington Northern Railroad.

The more Wes talked, the more I felt like I was being transported into a different life and time, and I could now picture myself walking with a band of people, long ago, like some tribe, and these were my own relatives, my own kind, and we lived right here in the high mountains of Glacier and had for many millennia. It was almost like a vision.

Wes was now going on and on about how we could do Wiley and the Wild West kind of stuff, but I really needed to learn how to yodel, as that was part of the old Western style of singing, and I definitely had the voice for it, having a high range and all. He knew he could get us gigs, maybe even some festivals.

But I wasn't listening, for I could now see some of my people standing at the forest's edge in the darkness, not far away at all, and they were somehow beckoning me to join them, saying I didn't belong where I was and would be much happier with them, living as I was meant to live as my kind had for thousands, maybe millions of years.

Wes was now irritated, and his sharp voice brought me back to reality. I assured him I'd been listening and would consider it all, and I thought changing from bluegrass to authentic Western would be a great thing, even though I barely knew what I was saying.

Wes had to go home, but I suddenly wanted him to stay. I felt like I was losing my sense of boundaries, who I was, and there was something out there I didn't understand.

I, of course, didn't say anything about all this to him, I just tried to get him to talk more about yodeling. But he stood to go, saying his wife would be worrying about him if he was very late, and besides, for some reason, he felt uncomfortable out here in the dark, like maybe there was a bear out there or something.

I followed him inside, locking the door, then turning on the deck lights. Becky was watching some TV show and the kids were upstairs, and I wanted desperately to get everyone together, as if there was some natural disaster about to happen. I almost felt panicked.

I figured it was something mental going on, maybe discomfort from Wes talking about playing in big venues and all, so I went back into the kitchen and got a beer, thinking it would settle my nerves.

As I stood there, I looked out the window at the edge of the forest, and I swear I could see eyes shining in the dark. I sometimes would see eyeshine from deer and elk and other animals if they passed through the outside lights, but this was different because it was a good six feet or more off the ground and nowhere near the lights—and the eyes were red as blood.

I was stunned and went back into the living room. I never drink late at night like that, and Becky noticed, asking if I was OK. I told her I felt weird and had just seen strange eyes looking at the house from the forest. She laughed, went into the kitchen to look, then came back to her TV show, saying it had to be my imagination and maybe I shouldn't be drinking beer.

I went upstairs and looked out from our bedroom window, but saw nothing. We have a nice recliner there for reading, and I crawled onto that, pulled a blanket up over my face, and promptly went to sleep.

I dreamed—or was it a dream?—that I was again with my people, and we were traversing a large glacier, careful to not fall into a crevasse, and it was all very tense. We were fleeing from something, and my mother held my hand tightly, telling me not to look back. My father was ahead of us, and he carried a spear and was dressed in a huge black robe, and it was then I looked back. In the distance was a creature with a coat just like the robe, and I knew my father had killed one and made a coat from it.

I woke, half sick, and it took me forever to realize where I was. Becky was in bed sleeping and had left the night light on.

I got up and quietly walked to the bedroom window, looking out again at the forest, but saw nothing. It was four a.m., and there was no way I was going to be able to sleep, so I went downstairs and made a pot of coffee and started a batch of cinnamon rolls. Like I said, I liked to cook—it relaxed me, and boy, did I ever need relaxing after that dream.

I wanted to go drink my coffee on the deck and watch the stars, which I often did when getting up early, though my normal time was around six, nor four. But I was afraid, so I went back to the living room.

I sat there sipping my hot coffee, thinking. What was going on? It was then that I remembered the DNA test Becky had wanted me to take, thinking it would be fun for the kids to know more about their genetics. I'd laughed it off, knowing there's a lot of controversy about the accuracy of such things. Becky had found it funny when mine had come back with the results saying I was four percent Neanderthal.

Kim had later done some research, telling me that being Neanderthal wasn't at all what I'd thought and that a lot of people had Neanderthal genes. Archeologists were now finding evidence that the Neanderthal had been artistic and musical, and they believed that they had blue eyes and red hair. Kim said that maybe I should be proud of my Neanderthal blood, as it maybe helped make me a better musician. I liked her theory and found it somewhat comforting.

But archaeologists also believe that the Neanderthal were killed off by Homo sapiens, even though there had been some interbreeding. Was this the source of the dreams? Were we fleeing from a Neanderthal?

It didn't seem right, and what about the red eyeshine I'd seen? Did it have anything to do with the dream?

The cinnamon rolls were done and the sun was rising, so I took a roll and another cup of coffee out to the back deck. I was feeling much better, now fully awake, one good cup of coffee already in me and a hot cinnamon roll wafting its yummy smell, and for no reason at all, I remembered what Wes had said the night before.

I started yodeling—well, my idea of yodeling, I should say. What I lacked in technique I made up for in volume, the sound reverberating off the nearby hills. I was impressed at how loud it sounded, but then again, I'd never tried yodeling off the deck before. I hoped I hadn't wakened Becky and the kids. For some reason, maybe in contrast to the dream, it felt like a new start, a new day, and I felt optimism and even joy.

I was happy to not be that kid hurrying across the glacier, being chased by something ominous, but instead here in beautiful Montana with a beautiful family and nice house and stunning landscape to look at whenever I wanted, and heck, I even liked my job. Life couldn't get any better.

Well, that's when the yodel came back to me, and no, it wasn't an echo. But it didn't sound human, nor was it really a yodel, but more of a strange yell coming from up the mountainside.

I quickly went back inside, shocked. In all the years we'd lived there, I'd never heard anything like that. And no, it wasn't a mountain lion, I'd heard plenty of those, as well as bobcat screams and even bears and coyotes making strange noises, as well as odd-sounding birds.

I again thought of the dream, and I somehow wondered if it was related. I again had the urge to gather my family and our two cats and flee, but now it was broad daylight, so it had nothing to do with strange night fears.

Becky was now up, having coffee and a roll, and I asked her if she'd heard anything. She hadn't, but wanted to go out on the deck and listen, intrigued by my description.

And of course we heard nothing out there at all. But we did have a nice discussion about moving into town, one instigated by me. Becky said I needed to get out of the house, and since it was Saturday, once the kids were up, we all went into Kalispell, where we had lunch and did a little shopping out at the mall north of town. I wanted to drive around a few neighborhoods, which made Becky realize that I was somewhat serious about moving.

I found several places I liked, but none had the views and privacy our place had. But now Becky started getting into the idea, as it would make work much closer for her, as she worked there in town. The kids were more hesitant, as it would mean changing schools, though neither had long until they were in college, and Kalispell has a community college they could both attend for their first two years, saving a bundle on tuition and other costs.

The idea was beginning to jell, and all because of red eyeshine, a dream, and an odd yell, none of which had been more than 24 hours earlier. I thought of all the work I'd put into our place, all the custom this and that, and I started feeling a sense of regret for having said anything. But we'd lived in the same place since before the kids were born, and we could get a fortune for it, especially with all that land, so maybe it wasn't such a bad idea.

But now Becky was saying something about how maybe we should leave Montana and try someplace new where we could buy a ranch for what our place was worth, like Wyoming or Nebraska. I knew she was thinking of her lifelong dream to live on a ranch like the one she'd grown up on instead of dealing with Medicare and Medicaid billing and non-paying patients all day long.

I couldn't believe where a weird dream and some strangeness was now heading. I loved Montana and never wanted to leave, it was where I'd been born and raised, and I was seriously regretting having said anything. Moving to a different property was one thing, but leaving Montana?

That evening, back on the deck, I was looking at things with new eyes, as if I'd just moved there, seeing it for what it was. They say you don't appreciate what you have until it's gone, and I didn't want that to happen. I wanted to look at what we had through unbiased eyes before we made any decisions. Sure, it had been my idea, but I now felt I'd been operating from a position of irrational fear.

I surveyed the scene—a beautiful pristine forest with wildlife galore, many who came to visit in the evening hours, unafraid. There were a number of animal trails we could walk in total peace and privacy, though we didn't go out there as much as we'd done when the kids were little, exploring and enjoying nature. And we even had our own small stream that coursed down through the forest from the big hills above us.

If I stood up or looked out from the upstairs windows, I could even see some of the high peaks in Glacier National Park towering high above with their snowcapped tops, a sight many would pay a fortune to have. And it was all so peaceful.

And what about the house? I'd built it with my own two hands while Becky and I lived in a small trailer. The cabinets were custom birch, and the ceilings were custom woods from a reclaimed flour mill over on the plains. Everything was handmade, and based on the praise I'd received over the years, well done. How could we ever sell it?

I felt a poignancy, a feeling that something important was about to be lost, and I went back inside. I needed to talk to Becky.

But when I saw her on her computer looking at some land agency's listings, I felt selfish and defeated. Maybe we should move for her sake. Sure, I'd built up a reputation as a finish carpenter, but I could rebuild that, even if we weren't in a well-heeled place. Becky had always been there for me, working hard at a job she really didn't like, and maybe it was time to give her a break. I just couldn't believe how fast things were moving.

That night, I had another dream. I was no longer a child, but I was still with my people, and now I was the one wearing the dark skin. I didn't really want to wear it, but my father was dead, killed by one of the black creatures. I now had to follow tradition and wear the robe.

And now, that creature's kin wanted to kill me. I could hear them in the nearby forest, talking in their strange language, and I knew they were coming for me.

All I wanted was to stop this killing and retribution. Why couldn't we live in peace? We were different, yet we had many similarities—we had language, loved our families, and ate the same plants and fish and small animals. It seemed we had much in common, so why fight? And I somehow knew my species would win in the end, decimating theirs, and this made me sad, even though they'd killed my father. I knew they were no Neanderthal.

Then, still dreaming, I wondered, did they have music? Did their brains process sound the same way ours did? Could their ears hear the many changes in pitch ours did? I'd read that humans can easily detect frequencies as fine as one twelfth of an octave—a half step in musical terminology—but predatory species such as dogs can only discriminate one third of an octave, and even our primate relatives could only hear changes of half an octave.

Were these black creatures primates like us? They had to be. Maybe music could be our common language, a way to communicate our fears and dreams to each other, and then we'd stop fighting.

I now dreamed that I took out a simple flute I'd carved and started playing. But they were still stalking me, and I stopped playing, getting my spear ready.

I woke, immediately knowing I'd been dreaming and yet afraid anyway. It all seemed too real, but Becky was beside me, sound asleep. It was four a.m., just like before.

I quietly got up and slipped on my clothes, then went downstairs to the kitchen, again making coffee. We still had some scones from the bakery in Kalispell the day before, so I grabbed one and went back on the deck, even though it was still pitch dark. I knew I had to confront my fears.

And there, again, like before, was something standing at the edge of the trees, something with glowing red eyes. I was scared to death and went back inside, but then I decided to get my fiddle. The dream had planted a thought—could music be a bridge between different species? I didn't even know what species I was looking at, but it was worth a try. Instead of running like a scared rabbit, I would give it a shot.

I began playing quietly, so as not to wake Becky and the kids, but hopefully loud enough that whatever was out there would hear me. I started out with an old Scottish song about the heather in the highlands and pining for a lost love, then segued into a beautiful Robert Burns song with Gaelic lyrics I didn't understand, something about calling the sheep.

I next thought of Wes and his desire to play old cowboy songs, so I played a song called *Twilight on the Trail*, then went into an old tune called the *Rose Blossom Special*. I must say I surprised myself at how many songs I actually knew.

And as I played, I wondered if whatever was out there would hear things the same way I did. Maybe they hated music and would run away.

When I finally looked up, the eyeshine was gone, but in its place were three shadows, and I thought at first they were bears, but soon realized I was looking at the same type of creatures I'd seen in my dreams. They were much closer, seemingly entranced by my playing.

It was almost dawn, just light enough to see them, and even though I knew I should be afraid, I wasn't, for I knew they wouldn't harm me. They nodded their heads as if asking for more, so I stood and played my heart out, every song I knew, from Marty Robbins to Blue Rodeo to Driftwood Holly and songs I've now long forgotten.

As the sun rose, they faded back into the trees, gone like a dream. And later that night, once it was again dark, I went back out onto the deck to find a beautiful bunch of colorful river stones on the steps, and I somehow knew they'd left them.

That same day, I called a land conservation agency and asked about putting most of our land into a perpetual conservancy, leaving only a couple of acres out for the house. I was worried that it would greatly decrease the amount we'd get from the property, but the guy there said it usually had the opposite effect, that it made it more desirable because the taxes were much lower and people liked knowing it would never be developed.

I talked to Becky and she was all for it, so we proceeded. After that was put into place, our next step was to call a real-estate agent and list the property. We were both astounded by what they suggested we list it for. Because it backed to Glacier National Park, it was worth a fortune, and we had several offers the week it was listed.

After we sold it, I was sitting on the back deck one last time, as we would leave the next morning, most of our stuff already moved to the place we'd rented in Kalispell until we could decide where to go next.

I'd left the band, no longer having any desire to play for an audience, for who could ever best the one I'd just played for?

There on the deck, I took out my fiddle and played an old Bob Marley tune, singing quietly, "Every little thing's gonna be alright."

I sat for awhile, enjoying the quiet, then went inside, turning off the deck lights for the last time.

ABOUT THE AUTHOR

Rusty Wilson is a fly-fishing guide based in Colorado and Montana. He's well-known for his Dutch-oven cookouts and campfires, where he's heard some pretty wild stories about the creatures in the woods, especially Bigfoot.

Whether you're a Bigfoot believer or not, we hope you enjoyed this book, and we know you'll enjoy Rusty's many others, the first of which is *Rusty Wilson's Bigfoot Campfire Stories*. Also check out Rusty's bestselling *Yellowstone Bigfoot Campfire Stories,* as well as *Bigfoot: The Dark Side*, *The Creature of Lituya Bay,* and *Chasing After Bigfoot: My Search for North America's Most Elusive Creature.*

Rusty's books come in ebook format, as well as in print and audio.

You'll also enjoy the first book in the Bud Shumway mystery series, a Bigfoot mystery, *The Ghost Rock Cafe.*

Other offerings from Yellow Cat Publishing include an RV series by RV expert Sunny Skye, which includes *Living the Simple RV Life.* And don't forget to check out the books by Sunny's friend, Bob Davidson: *On the Road with Joe*, and *Any Road, USA.* And finally, you'll love Roger Dean Miller's comedy thriller, *Bombing Hoffman.*

Made in the USA
Monee, IL
11 August 2020